Ride Like the Wind

Patricia Leitch started riding when a friend persuaded her to go on a pony trekking holiday – and by the following summer she had her own Highland pony, Kirsty. She wrote her first book shortly after this and writing is now her full-time occupation, but she has also done all sorts of different jobs, including being a riding-school instructor, groom, teacher and librarian. She lives in Renfrewshire, Scotland, with a bearded collie called Meg.

Other pony books in Armada by Patricia Leitch

A Horse for the Holidays
The Horse from Black Loch
Dream of Fair Horses
Jump to the Top

'Jinny' series

For Love of a Horse
A Devil to Ride
The Summer Riders
Night of the Red Horse
Gallop to the Hills
Horse in a Million
The Magic Pony

More 'Jinny' books will be published in Armada

Ride Like the Wind

Patricia Leitch

Armada

AN ORIGINAL ARMADA

Ride Like the Wind was first published in Armada in 1983
by Fontana Paperbacks,
8 Grafton Street, London W1X 3LA.

Printed in Great Britain by
William Collins Sons & Co. Ltd, Glasgow

CHAPTER ONE

The dream gripped Jinny Manders, pulling her down into its depths. Although she struggled to wake, as a drowning swimmer fights for air, it held her down in the place where there was nothing but a nameless, total, terror. An evil force crashed about her, and Jinny held up her arms to drive it away. But she was not strong enough. There was nothing she could do against it. She cowered away, still screaming; felt the ground move beneath her feet, so that there was no place of safety in the whole universe, and nowhere for Jinny to be except curled into herself, wrapped in her own screaming fear forever.

Jinny woke smothered in a web of her own long red hair, the echoes of her screaming still disturbing the security of her bedroom. For seconds she lay pinned down by the memory of her dream, then slowly let her gaze slide round her room. Nothing had changed, all was as it should be, dim in the early grey light of a summer morning.

Then Jinny thought of the horses. She leapt from her bed to the window in one panic-swift movement. Vivid in her mind's eye was the morning last spring when she had woken, gone to her window as she always did to call a greeting to Shantih, her beloved chestnut Arab, and looked out on to an empty field. But this morning the horses were all there – Jinny's Arab, Bramble, a solid black Highland the Manders borrowed from Miss Tuke's trekking centre, and Easter, an aged white pony whom Jinny had saved from a cruel riding school. They were all safe. Jinny sat down on the edge of her bed, too scared that she might fall back into her dream to risk going to sleep again. Even to think about it dragged her back into its power. She shivered uncontrollably. "Don't let it happen," she thought. "Please don't let it happen." But she didn't know what it was she was afraid of, what it was she dreaded.

"Now look here, Jinny Manders," she told herself, speaking aloud to hear the normality of her own voice. "Stop all this nonsense. You've finished with school for six whole weeks. Weeks and weeks of freedom and here you are getting your knickers in a knot because of a stupid dream."

But the darkness was still there. All the things on the surface of Jinny's life were as good as they had always been since her family — Jinny's mother and father, Petra, Jinny's sixteen-year-old sister, and Mike her ten-year-old brother — had left their city lives behind them in Stopton and come to live in Finmory House, a grey stone house that stood alone, four-square between the moorland and Finmory Bay. But now, underneath the surface of things, there was an uneasiness, a sense of autumn in the summer air that wouldn't leave Jinny alone. Although she hardly knew what it was, it followed on her heels like a shadow, was always there under the surface of her mind.

"Can't think about it here," Jinny decided and knew what she would do. She would go down to the horses and tell Shantih, her Arab, the things that were worrying her. Shantih would understand.

Jinny scrambled quickly into her clothes but before she left her bedroom she went through the archway that divided her room. The window in this part of the room looked out over the moors to where mountains shouldered up against the sky. The walls were covered with Jinny's drawings and paintings. There was a table and a chair, in

8

term time used for Jinny's reluctant homeworking but now holding paints, pastels and piles of paper.

On the wall was a mural of a red horse. It had been there, painted on the wall, waiting for Jinny when she had arrived at Finmory two years ago. Jinny and an old tinker woman had repainted it and now it stared out at Jinny, harsh and bright, its yellow eye commanding as a collie's eye. It was a being of power, held a strange magic force that linked Jinny to her own depths; but this morning it was too close to Jinny's nightmare.

She turned swiftly away from it, skeltered down the steep ladder of stairs that led from her room to the long upstairs corridor. She sped past doors that closed in her sleeping family, down the main flight of stairs, along the hall to the stone-flagged kitchen and out through the back door.

The world was without life, waiting, breath indrawn.

"My world," thought Jinny as she ran through wet grass, down past the stable, feed house and tack room that had been decaying outbuildings when the Manders had first arrived at Finmory. On she went, down to the horses' field, sea in front of her, glimpsed metallic and glittering between the black jaws of rock that held Finmory Bay within their bite.

"A dewdrop world that could vanish in a split second — all my family doing safe, correct things. Petra playing her piano, passing her music exams; Mike over the moon because Mr. MacKenzie is letting him drive his tractor; and me — Jinny and her pony."

As she ran, Jinny saw herself as if she were the beginning of a film where a skinny girl with long red hair ran through the grey morning, not knowing that these were the last moments of her old life; that in a moment the necessary action of the film would change everything, carrying her on against her will into an unknown future where nothing would ever be the same again.

"We have so much," Jinny thought. "Mountains and sea and freedom. So much. We're not real in our fairy-tale world."

But Shantih waiting at the field gate was real. No dream horse, but the Arab who had once been billed in a circus as a killer horse and now belonged to Jinny. She had found a bit in a book about a sheikh praising his Arab horse and it was how Jinny felt about Shantih. "Her face is a lamp uplifted to guide the faithful to the place of Allah."

Jinny flung herself over the gate and threw her arms round Shantih's neck, pressing her face against the warm bulk of horse.

"Dear horse," she murmured. "Dear real horse." And the threatening shadow of her nightmare drew back a little as Shantih turned her head and blew sweet-scented breath over Jinny's neck.

Easter, the white pony, lay flat on her side, spindle legs stretched from the coarse-coated barrel of her body. Her quarters and shoulders were no more than bones beneath her skin. Her long neck, almost without muscle, looked as if there was not enough strength in it to lift her fine-boned head from the ground. Only her tail and mane, lovingly brushed by Jinny into silver cascades of hair, showed no sign of the extreme age that blurred away the last traces of the top-class show pony that Easter had once been. At first, when Jinny had brought her from the Arran Riding School, Easter had flourished, and Jinny had been filled with the certainty that Easter had a long retirement ahead of her — summer days grazing with Shantih and Bramble, winter nights bedded down in deep straw while the gales stormed outside her thick stable walls.

"Blooming miracle she's still alive," the vet had said

when he had wormed Easter. "Forty if she's a day. Hardly worth worming her."

"But she is so much better," Jinny had declared.

"Give her a last summer and then . . ." the vet had said, leaving his death sentence unfinished.

"Don't talk nonsense. Easter's going to live at Finmory for years."

Then Jinny had been certain, but now she could hardly bear to look at the pony as she stood long hours without moving, head hanging, hardly bothering to even pick at the grass. She had refused all Jinny's offerings of treacle-laced bran mashes, oats mixed with chopped apple, milk pellets or sugar beet begged from Mr. MacKenzie whose farm was close to Finmory. Even when Jinny had grated a plateful of carrots for her, Easter had only breathed over it then walked slowly away.

Jinny pressed her face harder against Shantih's shoulder to blot out the thought of Easter, for surely, surely she had earned just one summer at Finmory to make up for the life she had led at the riding school.

Bramble stood close beside Easter. He was solid as a tank, self-willed and dour. When Easter had first been turned out into the field at Finmory, Bramble had welcomed her with gusty whickerings and urgent neck-nibblings. Jinny was sure that at some time in their past lives they had known each other. Now they were always together.

"But not for much longer," Jinny thought, turning to face the ponies, leaning back against Shantih's shoulder.

For most of the year Bramble lived at Finmory and Mike rode him to school in Glenbost village, but during the summer holidays Bramble went back to Miss Tuke and resumed his true role of trekking pony.

"Perhaps this year she'll forget. It will be September

11

before Tukey remembers, and we'll all be back at school."

"But of course we don't mind keeping him. Really we look on him as ours already," said Jinny, speaking to Miss Tuke inside her head.

"Strange you should say that. Just decided I'd give him to you. From now on he is yours. Bramble Manders."

"But how very kind," said Jinny's voice.

"Don't," Jinny warned herself. "Don't go on. It's not true."

Jinny knew that it was more likely for Shantih to grow wings than for Miss Tuke to give Bramble away. Any day now the phone would ring and Miss Tuke's foghorn voice would be telling Jinny it was time that black beggar was doing some honest work for a change.

"But Easter will miss him so much. What will she do without him?"

But Jinny had no answer.

She walked slowly across to the ponies. Bramble bustled to meet her, nudging her pocket, hoping for a titbit.

"Wait your hurry," Jinny told him, pushing him away. "You'll soon have dozens of trekkers to spoil you. You can bully them to your heart's content but not me."

Bramble swung round, ears pinned back, turning his quarters against Jinny.

"Get on with you," said Jinny sharply.

"As if I would," said Bramble, turning to face Jinny again, pricking his ears and instantly changing his expression from Roman-nosed ferocity to dish-faced innocence.

"Clown," said Jinny, giving him a bit of carrot from her pocket.

At Jinny's approach, Easter had lifted her head and was

watching Jinny through dull, lack-lustre eyes. Jinny crouched down on the grass beside her, gently stroking the gaunt head, dry ears and the harsh hollowness of her neck under its long mane. She dug into her pocket offering Easter sugar lumps and carrot, but Easter moved her head away with a small movement of rejection and a cold tightness settled in Jinny. She got to her feet and stood looking down at the pony. She wasn't getting any better.

Suddenly Easter surged upwards, forelegs stretched awkwardly in front of her she strained for purchase. For a long moment she balanced there then, with a final struggle, she lifted herself and stood with her head hanging. She took a few steps away from Jinny and began to pluck listlessly at the grass.

Instantly Jinny was filled with hope. Easter was only old, had only been resting.

The sound of Shantih's hooves made Jinny look round. Ken Dawson was standing at the field gate, Kelly, his grey dog, lying beside him.

Ken Dawson lived with the Manders. He was eighteen, tall and angular with fair, shoulder-length hair. Every month his rich parents sent him a cheque but, apart from that, they had nothing to do with him. Jinny went cold when she thought about it — your own parents not loving you.

In his kitchen garden Ken grew all the fruit and vegetables that the Manders needed. Ken was a vegetarian, eating nothing that came from animals. "How can you say you love animals when you slaughter days-old calves so you can drink the milk that was meant for them?" And to this Jinny had no answer. She knew what Ken said was true.

Ken stood at the gate causing no stir, no disturbance. If Petra had been standing there her eyes would have been

13

accusing Jinny of fecklessness, of untidyness. Her father, even standing still, would only have been pausing from getting on with something more important. But Ken was there, being not doing.

"Manders on the move," said Ken, as Jinny climbed over the gate to stand beside him. "Tom's up making himself tea. You down here. On the stir, all of you."

Jinny knew only too well why her father was up so early. She pushed the thought out of her head, for this was the blackest of all the things that waited restlessly under the surface of Jinny's life.

"Easter's up too," she said hurriedly. "And she's grazing."

Ken nodded, not saying as almost anyone else would have done that the few blades of grass held between Easter's slack lips could hardly be called grazing.

Colour had come back into the world – greens of myriad shades; the sea, turquoise ice, knife-grey, the sky so space-blue there was no lid on the world.

"What's Tom going to do if they send his book back again?"

A time warp from her dream engulfed Jinny. For a moment outside the present the ground moved under her feet. There was nowhere for her to stand.

"Of course they won't send it back. Of course they won't," she almost shouted. "They only wanted him to make a few changes in it, and he's done that. When they read it this time, it will be exactly what they want."

"And if it's not?" asked Ken, turning to look straight at Jinny. "If they won't publish it, what then?"

"He'll go on making pots, selling them to Nell, the way you've always done."

Mr. Manders had been a probation officer in Stopton but, when they had come to live at Finmory, he had become a potter, selling his work to Nell Storr who owned a craft shop in Inverburgh, their nearest town. He had also written a book about the conditions which destroyed young people living in a place like Stopton. It had been a success, selling foreign rights and having a television documentary based on it. A month ago his publishers had sent his second manuscript back to him, wanting part of it changed. Mr. Manders had changed it and returned it to them. Like Jinny, he was waiting for a letter.

"Tom go on being a potter?" mused Ken. "It's not how he sees himself now. His pots are a hobby. He sees himself as someone who can get things changed through his books; a sand witch fingering the dreams of others, shaping destiny, does our Tom."

Jinny didn't answer. She still didn't really see her father as a person to be criticized. He was her father and that was that. In a way she didn't want Ken to speak about him like that, in a way it fascinated her.

"They won't send it back," said Jinny.

"If you say so," said Ken.

They walked down to the sea, Kelly feathering ahead of them, turning bright eyes through the denseness of his hair to check that they were still with him. Where the sea drew back from the sand it left a shimmering stretch of white light; dazzling, moving quicksand. As they walked over it, each step they took left dark prints, yet when Jinny glanced back the shining level was smooth again; no trace remained of the way they had taken.

"I'd a nightmare," began Jinny, breaking the silence. "I dreamt..." and then she couldn't go on. She couldn't remember what she had dreamt, couldn't find words to tell Ken.

Breakfast was over before they heard the sound of the postman's van.

15

Mr. Manders went to the door and came back in with a parcel. It was from his publishers. They had sent his book back.

They all waited while he opened the parcel, laid his typescript on the table and took a letter from an envelope, reading it quickly to himself before he read part of it aloud.

"'. . . and taking into account these varied opinions we have decided that your manuscript, as it stands at present, is not suitable for publication. Should you feel able to make major changes along the lines we have indicated, we would be more than willing to reconsider it.

Yours sincerely,
Stephen Jones.'

"I met Stephen when I went to London," said Mr. Manders, glancing up. "He's added a hand-written PS. 'For myself, I found parts of your book stimulating and insightful. A common criticism, which I must say I shared, was that it lacked the immediacy of your first work which was so obviously alive with personal experience of the teenagers you were writing about. In chapter five you comment at some length on an act which is no longer in force. A minor point, but seized upon by those who gave your book the thumbs down.'

"And that," said Mr. Manders, "is that. The thumbs down."

"Would it be quite impossible to change it?" asked Mrs. Manders.

"Totally. They don't want it changed. It would be a complete rewrite, and I can't do that."

"It can't be as good as your last one," said Petra, wiping down the draining board with smug efficiency.

Jinny glowered through her hair at her sister, hating the way she shone with cleanliness. Her hair was neat and tidy, her clothes were crisp and smart. "Bad enough having your book sent back, without Petra going on at you," she thought.

"The maddening thing is," went on Mr. Manders, "they're right in what they say. It is years since I had anything to do with Stopton kids. Stuck out here in this wilderness."

Jinny turned away quickly. She went down to the stable, took Shantih's bridle and went on down to the field. She bridled Shantih, not looking too hard at where Easter was standing dozing in the shade of the hedge, and springing up on to Shantih's back, rode her past Finmory and over the moors.

Jinny touched her legs against Shantih's sides and felt her surge forward into a gallop. Their speed wiped Jinny's mind clear. There was nothing but this ecstasy of space. Jinny rode centaur-like, growing from her horse; Shantih's strength and power her own, all the glory her own. Loose stones clipped beneath Shantih's beating hoofs, heather roots and bracken had no hold against her. The track of air she followed lifted over stone walls and burns running peat-clear through the heather. Jinny rode like the wind.

At last Jinny steadied Shantih to a walk, slackened her reins, clapped her hard neck. There would always be Shantih.

"Fire horse," praised Jinny. "Desert dancer. Joy of my being."

She turned Shantih and stood looking out over the folded sweeps of moorland and suddenly, in the mid-distance, there was a girl riding a black horse. Jinny stared in blank amazement. The girl was tall and slender, dressed for riding in expensive jodhpurs, boots and black jacket. The sun glinted on blonde hair beneath her hard hat. It was certainly not Claire Burnley, and Claire Burnley was the only other person who might have been riding on the moors.

Jinny opened her mouth to shout to the girl but for seconds only a croak of sound came out.

"Hi!" Jinny yelled, finding her voice at last. "Hi, wait a minute. Hi!"

Shantih flinched at the noise, but the girl never looked round. She cantered on, away from Jinny. In another moment she would be out of sight.

"Wait for me!" Jinny roared and clapped her heels against Shantih's sides. The Arab reared, and Jinny clutched at insubstantial handfuls of mane.

"Stupid idiot! It's Shantih you're on, not Bramble," Jinny told herself as she fought to stay on top of Shantih, to urge her on as Shantih's forefeet touched down. But she couldn't manage it. Shantih's neck disappeared, head tucked between knees. Her quarters bulked skywards. Her hind hooves lashed out at the sun, and Jinny shot from her back and crashed down into the heather.

When Jinny scrambled to her feet, both girl and horse had gone. The moor was empty again.

CHAPTER TWO

Jinny rode home through Mr. MacKenzie's yard and, hearing Shantih's hoofbeats, Mr. MacKenzie emerged from the byre.

"Guess what I saw on the moors," Jinny called.

"A fancy bit lassie riding a black horse," he said, fixing Jinny with the gimlet gaze of his washed-blue eyes.

"Typical," exclaimed Jinny. "I might have known you'd be sitting on a wall watching."

"Is it yourself has been at the hibernation not to have heard the news?"

"Tell me. I haven't heard a thing."

"Have you not heard it is the rich strangers we have staying at Hawksmoor? Friends of the banker man who owns it. The Mr. Dalton is a fat old gnome with the chain of discos raging away all over England, and his wife is an old boiler done up like a spring chicken. But the lassie, Kat Dalton she is after calling herself, will be ages with yourself, I'm thinking, and as wasted, being driven up here in a brand new horsebox. They're saying it is the racehorse she has, those that have seen it."

"Could be," said Jinny, seeing the black horse in her mind's eye. "Looked fast enough."

"No doubt you will be finding out for yourself."

"Well," said Jinny. The summer holidays stretched before her to be lived through without Sue. Sue Horton, Pippen, her pony, and her parents had camped at Finmory Bay last summer. This year they were going to Greece.

"And if it is not yourself that is chiselling them out, I'm

thinking they will be knocking at your door themselves."

"Why?" said Jinny, thinking it unlikely when they were rich enough to buy their daughter a horsebox with a racehorse inside it.

"Mr. Dalton was in Mrs. Simpson's shop telling her the terrible problems he has getting rid of his money before the tax man pounces. Does he not spend his holidays going round the Highlands looking for the likely houses to buy, offers the big money for them, does them up fancy and sells them again. And leaves the poor tax man fair muddled with it all. Or so he was after telling Mrs. Simpson."

"But why would that make him come to Finmory?"

"With the cash in his hand. It's the fair notion he has taken to the place. Wasn't he asking Mrs. Simpson the Mastermind questions about you all."

"Dad would never sell Finmory."

"And him with his new book like the homing pigeon?"

"Honestly!" exclaimed Jinny in disgust. "I do not know how you find things out."

"It's the big money he would be offering for Finmory."

"No," said Jinny. "Definitely no."

When Jinny told her family about the Daltons, Mr. Manders said, "Dalton? Dalton's Discos. There was one in Stopton. Wonder if it is the same lot."

"He wants to buy a holiday house here. Told Mrs. Simpson that he liked Finmory!" and Jinny waited for her father's indignant laughter. "Imagine thinking he could buy Finmory!"

But Mr. Manders didn't laugh.

"He would pay something for Finmory," he said.

His words laid icy fingers along Jinny's spine for they

20

weren't casual, paper-handkerchief words. He was speaking directly to her mother, meaning what he said.

The next morning Jinny rode Shantih towards Hawksmoor.

"I'm not actually going to have anything to do with them," she told herself. "But if it *is* a racehorse. . . And the girl might be O. K. She doesn't have to be like her family."

Hawksmoor lay in the opposite direction to Glenbost village, so that Jinny seldom passed it. Even when she was riding that way she hardly ever went along the narrow road that led to Hawksmoor, for it stopped at Hawksmoor's high iron gates, didn't go anywhere else. The house belonged to an English banker who came up sometimes to shoot things, then went back to England taking the creatures he had killed with him.

Shantih was fresh — her head high, her tail lifted and her trotting hooves drumming the road, desperate to be galloping.

"We are not," Jinny told her severely, sitting down hard in the saddle and turning her up the road to Hawksmoor. "This is a road ride, control yourself."

But Shantih danced sideways, challenging the silence through trumpeting nostrils. A sheep erupted from the roadside, her grown lamb bleating behind her. Shantih leapt into the air. Four feet off the ground, she humped her back and starfished skywards. Jinny dug her knees into the saddle rolls and gripped the pommel to stay on top.

The car coming down the road towards them hardly slowed down. Jinny just managed to control Shantih before it drew level with her. A bald man was driving it. The woman sitting next to him was wearing a dress of purple silk, so obviously expensive and fashionable that even Jinny noticed it. In the back of the car was a girl with straight, shoulder-length fair hair cut in a long fringe. As the car passed Jinny, the driver sounded his horn. Shantih leapt the ditch at the side of the road and in a mad flurry of fear, half real, half used as an excuse for a gallop, she was storming over the moors with Jinny crouched over her neck totally out of control.

At last, swinging her round in wide circles, Jinny managed to bring Shantih to a halt.

"Idiot mare," she told her guiltily, knowing that it was weeks and weeks since she had schooled Shantih, and that Shantih had been slipping steadily back into her old tearaway madness. But Jinny had been too worried about Easter to do anything about it. When she had been riding Shantih all she had wanted to do was to gallop, urging Shantih on to greater speed to help her leave her worries behind.

"Making a fool of me like that," Jinny muttered, jumping to the ground. "They were the Daltons. He's the man who thinks he can buy Finmory. Just the kind of thing he would do, blasting his horn when he was passing us. You could have broken a leg or anything, getting a fright like that. And that girl staring at me!"

From where she stood, Jinny looked down on to Hawksmoor House — its Sleeping Beauty tangle of overgrown grounds, its stone turrets surfacing from the surge of ivy, lay beneath her. But although it looked neglected from the outside, Jinny knew that the banker had renovated the inside, bringing up an interior decorator from London to design it for him.

"Huge place," thought Jinny, imagining herself living there. She would take Bramble, Easter and Shantih inside with her. She imagined the horses and herself eating from the same table, sitting round the fire at night while the gales stormed over the moors.

But today it was summer sky and sun. Both Mr. and Mrs. Dalton and their daughter had been in the car, and if there was anyone working for them they would be from the village and Jinny would know them. Without actually admitting to herself what she was planning to do, Jinny remounted and turned Shantih down towards Hawksmoor.

Both gates stood wide open. Jinny hesitated.

"Even if they are only going into Glenbost they won't be back yet," Jinny told herself. "And I'm not doing any harm, only looking."

Jinny straightened her shoulders, flicked back her hair and rode Shantih determinedly up the drive. Pine trees lined an avenue that led straight up to Hawksmoor's steps. Shantih walked light-hoofed on a dense carpet of decaying pine needles.

Heart in her mouth, Jinny rode past the house and round to the outbuildings at the back. Shantih's head came up, with goggling eyes she looked about her, then with a trembling whicker of sound she carried Jinny round the side of a broken-paned greenhouse and into a neglected stable yard. On one side were what had once been tack rooms and feedhouses, but now doors hung from their hinges, crookedly awry; nettles and dockens invaded rotten wooden floors. But on the other side of the yard, from one of the decaying looseboxes, a black head looked out. Shantih kinked her tail and pranced on the spot, blowing through wide nostrils.

"Steady," warned Jinny. "Steady Shantih." But all her attention was taken up by the black mare. She had a white star, a fringing of pulled mane, a wisp of forelock, and the sweetest, most gentle expression that Jinny had ever seen in a horse. Her thoroughbred head lacked the carven quality of Shantih's dished Arab face. It seemed smooth and silken, a melting quality in her bones. Flames of white light glistered her satin coat as she moved, and ears, fit for silken purses, pricked with mild curiosity at the intruders.

Jinny slipped to the ground and spoke to the black horse, holding out her hand for the tickling caress of her velvet lips.

"Aren't you a beauty?" she said, running her outstretched hand down the mare's muscled neck. Her hard body gleamed jet in the shadows of the box. She was about sixteen hands high and finely built. Jinny didn't know enough about horses to be able to judge her conformation, but she knew instinctively that every line of the black horse was bred for speed. Standing still she was like an arrow held in a drawn bow, only waiting to be set free, to fly faster than the eye could follow.

"As fast as Shantih," Jinny thought, and for a second she was astride Shantih racing the black mare.

Suddenly Jinny realised how long she had been standing talking to the mare.

She said a hurried good-bye to her, promising to see her again soon. Then, mounting Shantih, she cantered down the drive, her nerves still jangling, expecting the Daltons' car to appear through the gates with every second. Even out on the road leading from Hawksmoor, Jinny hurried Shantih on.

Within minutes of turning on to the broader road the Daltons' car came into sight.

"Timing excellent," Jinny thought, congratulating herself as she turned Shantih off the road and on to the moor, just in case Mr. Dalton should sound his horn again.

The car sped towards her and again, to Jinny's fury, the

24

driver blasted his horn. Shantih half reared, but this time Jinny was ready for her. She steadied her, speaking soothingly, telling Shantih to pay no attention to such bad manners.

The woman sitting in the front twinkled scarlet nails at Jinny, but the girl stared from the back window with an expression of superior disdain on her face.

"Nasty little snob," thought Jinny, as she rode back home. "If I was somewhere and I saw a girl riding an Arab I'd be out of the car speaking to her. I'd be wanting to get to know her."

"She could have been shy," suggested Mrs. Manders, when Jinny told her about the meeting. "Perhaps she thought the same about you."

"That will be right," said Jinny. "She looked at me as if I'd just crawled out from under a stone."

"Probably thought you had," said Petra, "if you were wearing those jeans."

"Ha, bloomin' ha," said Jinny, refusing to be drawn. "And she has such a super horse. I think she really might be a racehorse."

"How do you know what her horse is like?" demanded Petra suspiciously.

"Saw her on the moors yesterday, didn't I?" said Jinny quickly and went out before her sister had time to ask any more questions.

Jinny mixed a small feed and took it down to Easter.

"Just eat a little," Jinny pleaded, holding it out hopefully to Easter.

The pony was dozing, standing with her eyes closed, head hanging. At the sound of Jinny's voice she started awake, coming back from some far place to find a bucket of food being held beneath her nose. Automatically she reached out to the feed, opened her mouth and then, just

25

when Jinny thought she was going to take a mouthful, she seemed to slip back into her dream and turned away without eating anything.

"Oh Easter, don't. Please eat something. You must eat."

Jinny tried feeding the pony from her hand, running the feed through her fingers and rattling the oats against the side of the bucket, but nothing she did made any difference.

"It's no use," thought Jinny. "I must get the vet. Dad will need to pay for him. There must be something he could do for her."

Yesterday evening Jinny had told her father that Easter would need to have the vet. Mr. Manders had grunted and gone on reading his book. When Jinny asked again, he told her not to make such a fuss, that the vet had seen Easter once and told Jinny that there was nothing he could do for the pony, that she was too old.

"I'll need to ask Miss Tuke," Jinny decided, but she didn't want to remind Miss Tuke of her existence. She wanted to lie low and keep Bramble for as long as she could. But she would need to ask Miss Tuke for advice and if she got in touch with Miss Tuke. . .

"That's how I think. Round and round in circles getting nowhere."

Jinny gave up trying to make Easter eat and tipped the feed out for Bramble.

"All right for some," she told him as he hoovered it down.

The phone rang while the Manders were having supper. Mr. Manders jumped to answer it. Petra raised her eyebrows at her mother.

"He phoned his publishers," said Mrs. Manders. "Stephen Jones is phoning him back this evening."

Before Jinny could ask any questions, her father called her to the phone.

"It's Miss Tuke for you. Don't be on all night. I'm expecting a call from London."

"Bet she wants Bramble back," Jinny thought dismally as she answered the phone.

"Jinny?" checked Miss Tuke's foghorn voice. "Good show. Now listen carefully. It's all fixed up. Tomorrow night. Six o'clock. You'll have heard that there's people staying at Hawksmoor? Dalton's their name. Arrived at my place tonight demanding cross-country instruction for the daughter. I told him Saturdays were my only free days while we were trekking, and he offers me fifteen pounds for an hour's instruction, so I'm taking her tomorrow night."

"So what," thought Jinny. "I don't care what Kat Dalton is doing."

"Next he demands company for his daughter. I suggest Sara and Pym, but when the girl heard Pym is a Highland pony she said he wouldn't be fast enough. You were acceptable. They liked the sound of an Arab."

"I can't pay fifteen pounds!" exclaimed Jinny.

"They are paying for you."

"But ..." objected Jinny, not at all sure that she liked the idea of being paid for. "I don't ..."

"My cash flow needs all the fifteen pound booster shots it can get. You're coming. No excuses. Give you some competition. Sharpen you up. You've to phone them. Glenbost 735."

Jinny found pencil and paper and wrote the number down.

"See you six o'clock," said Miss Tuke. "Be in good form. The girl is quite a rider. She told me so herself." And Miss Tuke put the phone down before Jinny had a chance to ask her about Easter. "But at least she never mentioned Bramble," Jinny thought as she put the receiver down.

She stood thinking about the way Kat Dalton had looked at her, the Daltons' road-hog killer car and the cheek of them, thinking they could buy Finmory. Jinny didn't want anything to do with the Daltons. She would phone Miss Tuke back, tell her she wasn't riding with Kat. Then Jinny remembered the black mare. She wanted to see her out of her box being galloped over the moors, wanted to race Shantih against her.

Jinny picked up the receiver and dialled the Daltons' number. A man's voice replied.

"Hullo," said Jinny. "I'm Jinny Manders. Miss Tuke told me to phone you."

"Hold on." Jinny heard the man shouting for Kat. Jinny waited.

Mr. Manders had come out of the kitchen and was standing beside Jinny and tapping his watch.

"I'm holding on," mouthed Jinny.

"Hard earned," said Mr. Manders, meaning the money that was paying for the phone call.

"Can't put it down now," said Jinny, scowling at her father.

"Hullo," said a girl's voice. "Kat Dalton here."

"It's Jinny Manders. Miss Tuke told me about riding with you."

Kat Dalton said nothing.

"Is it tomorrow night?" said Jinny, floundering. "She said I was to phone you about it, that you wanted me to have a lesson with you."

"It was Paul, actually. He's paying for you, isn't he? So I suppose it is all arranged. Will you ride over here? We'll box them to Miss Tuke's. Your horse will have been boxed before?"

Kat's voice was distant, supercilious; it held no interest or enthusiasm. It filled Jinny with instant dislike.

"Of course," said Jinny, wanting to tell this Kat Dalton that she didn't care if she never rode with her, never met her, that she wanted nothing to do with her.

"Be here for five," said Kat. "Oh, hold on a moment."

Jinny heard muffled voices and tried to look as if she was listening intently. It helped her to ignore her father's watch-tapping routine which was becoming more and more demented.

"Helen says you are to come for lunch. She says it will give us a chance to get to know each other. Be here for twelve, then we can ride in the afternoon. I'd like to see what your riding is like before we go to Miss Tuke's. Bye," and Kat hung up before Jinny had a chance to reply.

"About time," said her father.

"Rude!" exclaimed Jinny. "Rude and super rude! She must be the rudest person I've ever met. Like to see what my riding is like! That's what she said. She did. I've a jolly good mind not to go at all. Blooming cheek."

"You'd better do something about your appearance then," said Petra, when Jinny had finished giving her family a word by word account of her phone calls.

For once Jinny didn't argue.

"I'll wash my jodhs," she said, going to look for them.

CHAPTER THREE

"But whatever did you do to them?" Mrs. Manders exclaimed next morning, as Jinny held up a shrunken pair of jodhpurs for her inspection.

"I put them in the sink, sprinkled soap powder over them, poured in the boiling water and left them to soak. Is there nothing you can do to stretch them?"

"Nothing, I'm afraid."

"Then I shall need to go in my jeans. They will see me as a character."

"Oh, Jinny!" exclaimed Petra, coming in and viewing the shrunken jodhs with amazement.

"Cheap rubbish," said Jinny, disclaiming all responsibility. "They were too small anyway. I was always getting cleg bites in the gap between them and my jodh boots," and she went out to catch Shantih.

Easter was standing nose to tail with Bramble. Last night she had eaten a few more handfuls of feed but this morning she had turned her head away refusing to eat.

"Least I'll be able to ask Miss Tuke about her," Jinny thought, sitting down on the grass. "If Miss Tuke says I should get the vet, Dad can't argue with her. I'll get her to speak to him."

Jinny had no money to pay for the vet herself. Normally she could make money by selling her pictures to Nell Storr. Nell had bought eleven of Jinny's pictures so that she had been able to buy Easter, but last time Jinny had been in Nell's shop there were still four of her pictures left and Jinny didn't like to ask Nell to buy any more until they were all sold.

"Think of her well again," Jinny told herself. She tried to imagine Easter young again, bright-eyed, with rounded quarters and arched neck; tried to imagine the rosettes that must once have fluttered from her bridle. Jinny's imagination built the show ground around her — the smell of crushed grass, the hooves of the horses, the incredible striving for cups — and Jinny was sitting on Easter while the judge presented her with a red rosette.

Jinny went back to the stable, found the pad of paper and the pencil which she kept there and returned to the field. Staring at the real Easter, Jinny drew her as she must have been in her days of praise. Jinny was filled with the intuition that if she only knew the secret, her drawing could make Easter young again; could bring back taut muscle and satin coat; that there was some trick about time. It was a monkey god, an aging magician, and when Jinny drew she could see through his pathetic trick and, having seen that it was only a trick, she could re-shuffle time to suit herself, any way she wanted.

"You're not still here," said Mike. "Mum sent me to see if you'd gone without telling us. It's nearly eleven o'clock. If you've to get there for lunch you'll need to belt."

Jinny shuddered back to normality. She hadn't heard Mike coming across the field. If Mike hadn't disturbed her, could she have done it? Could she?

"That is terrific," said Mike, taking the drawing from Jinny. "It is Easter, only years ago when she was young."

Jinny would have hidden her drawing from almost anyone else. Ken, Nell and Mike were the only three who understood about her drawing, who didn't gush, embarrassing her.

"Not really eleven? Oh glory!" And Jinny, catching

Shantih by the forelock, bustled her out of the field and up to her box.

"Late," Jinny told her as she attacked her with a dandy-brush, scrubbing at muddied hocks and grass-stained legs. "Always late. Wanted to have you looking really special but I never manage it. Still, they'll see that we're not the type for Kat and that will be that."

Jinny dragged a body-brush through Shantih's mane and tail, took care over her saddle patch and elbows. Then, with final sweeping strokes from neck to quarters, she tacked her up and dashed into the house to get herself ready.

"Aren't you going to wear your jacket?" asked Mrs. Manders, catching Jinny as she was on her way out again.

"Too small," said Jinny. "It looks ridiculous. I keep telling you I need a new one."

"And that anorak is filthy," said Mrs. Manders as Jinny dashed past.

Catching Jinny's excitement, Shantih burst from her box. Tail kinked, head high, she whirled dervish-like around Jinny as she tried to tighten her girth.

"Stand still," beseeched Jinny, muffled under the flap of her saddle. "Shantih, stand still!"

Even when Shantih's girth was fastened and Jinny was trying to mount, Shantih refused to stand.

"What's up with her this morning?" asked Mike, coming to Jinny's rescue. "Haven't seen her messing about like this for ages." Mike caught hold of Shantih's bit ring just in time to stop her rearing.

"Don't know," lied Jinny, trying not to think about the huge feed she had given Shantih the night before to make sure that she would be fit for Miss Tuke's cross-country. "She's just fresh. I like her like this."

32

"Rather you then me," declared Mike, watching his sister as she was carried out of the yard and down the track to Mr. MacKenzie's on a prancing, plunging Shantih.

Jinny turned Shantih along the road that led to Hawksmoor.

"Never," said Shantih, forefeet tittuping, her weight sunk back on her quarters. "We never go that way."

"Oh yes we do," said Jinny, insisting with seat and hands, remembering just in time not to use her heels. "Get on with you."

Shantih spun round and charged into the farmyard, scattering hens and sending the farm dogs into hysterics.

"What would you be at now?" demanded Mr. MacKenzie, coming out from the hayshed.

"I'm going to Hawksmoor," Jinny shouted back, furious that the farmer should have seen her making such a fool of herself. "Shantih doesn't want to go."

Mr. MacKenzie grabbed a stick and advanced on them with waving arms.

"Don't hit her," warned Jinny, knowing from grim past experience that any kind of whip or stick brought back fearful memories of the circus, triggering Shantih into violent terror.

But Jinny was too late. Shantih had seen the stick. Jinny felt her horse bunch tight beneath her, then, head down, Shantih bolted from the yard at full gallop. Knees tight against her saddle, sawing at her reins, Jinny just managed to steer Shantih's crazy runaway in the direction of Hawksmoor. After that there was nothing she could do except sit tight.

They had almost reached the turning to Hawksmoor before Shantih began to slow down and pay any attention to the bit in her mouth or Jinny on her back.

"Oh, horse," mourned Jinny, when at last Shantih came to a walk and Jinny was able to jump to the ground. "It's all right. You'll never, ever go back to that circus. That's all past now," and Jinny turned Shantih, head into the wind, gazing in dismay at her lathered sides, foaming mouth and wild eyes.

Half an hour later, when Jinny was leading her up the drive to Hawksmoor, Shantih was still rust red with sweat; eyes rolling she pranced at Jinny's side. Ringmasters lurked behind every tree trunk, every branch was a whip.

"Wait till I see Mr. MacKenzie," Jinny thought grimly.

Before they reached Hawksmoor House, the door opened and Kat Dalton came down the steps. At least, Jinny supposed it must be Kat, for the person coming towards her had straight blonde hair cut in a long fringe above her black eyebrows, hair that fell in a curtain of glinting gold.

For seconds Jinny thought that this must be some relation of Kat's, maybe an older sister or aunt. She was wearing a white linen dress and jacket, gold sandals that were no more than high heels and a jewelled strip of leather. She was tanned a smooth honey-gold as if she had just been taken out from under a toaster, and her face was skilfully made up.

"Manders," thought Jinny, dismounting, "drop dead. Earth open and swallow me up."

Kat came slowly down the steps.

"It is you," she said. "You *are* in a muck sweat. Are you all right? When Miss Tuke said you had an Arab, I told Paul you would be the girl we'd seen from the car. Do you always gallop about like that?"

"She got a fright," muttered Jinny, scowling back at

Kat, on the defensive, thinking that Kat saw her as a stupid child who couldn't control her horse.

"Really? Is she nervous? She looks as if she would be. You'd better take her down to the stables. We've been waiting to start lunch." Kat led the way down the side of the house and round the greenhouse to the stable yard.

Shantih, remembering the black horse, pranced at Jinny's side, whinnying.

"Put her in there," said Kat, indicating the box next to her own horse. "I only hope she won't upset Lightning."

"She won't," snapped Jinny. "She's used to other horses."

"Really," said Kat, turning her back on Jinny.

"Go home," thought Jinny. "Just get back on Shantih and go home. She doesn't want me. I don't need to stay here and be spoken to like this."

But Jinny didn't. She took Shantih's tack off, gave her a quick wisp down and, telling her to behave herself, left her in the box.

"At last," said Kat. "Do come along." She turned nonchalantly on her six inch heels and began to walk back to the house.

Jinny paused to make sure that Shantih had water, then to stroke Lightning's gleaming neck, run the silken ears through her hands and scratch under the mare's neck.

"Do leave Lightning alone," Kat called, without looking back. "And don't feed sweets to her. Paul didn't pay six thousand for her to have you spoiling her."

"Spoiling her!" exclaimed Jinny indignantly, trotting after Kat, conscious of her muddied jodh boots, sweat-stained jeans, the sticky mess of her anorak sleeves where she had tried to dry Shantih's head, and the utter impossibility of anyone paying six thousand pounds for a

35

horse. "I wasn't going to feed her. You never even spoke to her."

Kat glanced back and, for a moment, it seemed to Jinny that her expression had changed, as if something that Jinny had said had touched a half-healed wound.

"If you knew what . . ." began Kat, but stopped herself almost before she had begun to speak. Her face hardened again. "I should think," she said, "you'd want to wash before lunch."

"And I said," repeated Jinny, catching up, "you never even spoke to her."

Kat turned, her hair a silken curtain, a swinging shampoo commercial. She opened her eyes wide, staring at Jinny, and her eyes under their black lashes were yellow as a cat's. Black eyebrows in sharp contrast to her blonde hair arched above them. She lifted pink-painted lips from the whitest teeth that Jinny had ever seen.

"And *I* said, I hoped you were going to wash before we had lunch."

Jinny did her best to clean herself up in the pale lemon cloakroom where Kat had left her. She took off her anorak, scrubbed her hands, arms and face; combed her hair with a huge comb that was lying beneath the mirror and was probably meant to be an ornament, and rubbed her jodh boots clean with toilet paper.

"We are waiting," said Kat's voice from the other side of the door.

Jinny ignored her. She was staring in dismay at the dirty footprints on the pale lemon carpet. There was nothing she could do about them.

"Don't care," she thought. "Don't care what they think about me. After today I'll never see them again." And Jinny picked up her anorak and walked out of the cloakroom, shutting the door quickly behind her so that

36

the footprints would be a surprise for whichever Dalton went into the cloakroom next.

The walls of the high hall and the corridor were encrusted with the heads of dead stags, foxes, roe deer and badgers. From the first landing a pair of stuffed, moth-eaten golden eagles peered down at them.

Kat opened a door, stood back so that Jinny had to go in first. Where the hall and corridor had been dark and old this room had been transformed into a Homes and Gardens confection. Walls, woodwork and carpet were white; huge easy chairs were covered in floral loose covers, and the wooden furniture was a light, good wood colour. For a second Jinny stood blinking in a haze of cigar smoke.

"Do come in," welcomed a female voice, and a slim woman eased herself gracefully from one of the chairs and came across to Jinny, glass in hand.

"This is Jinny. Jinny, this is Helen," introduced Kat.

"Kat is so pleased you are going to be riding with her," said Helen, holding out limp fingers.

"Hasn't been talking to Kat recently," thought Jinny as she grasped Helen's dead-fish hand.

"And Paul," said Kat, gesturing to where the cigar smoke was densest.

Sitting in the armchair was a bald, fat Humpty Dumpty. His legs stuck out in front of his egg-shaped body, hardly reaching the floor. The backs of his broad hands were carpeted with curling black hairs. His eyes, lost in their own reflections, stared blindly from behind pebble lenses. He had a squat nose and thick lips. On the arm of his chair was an empty brandy glass. When he shook hands with Jinny he held on to her too long. A moment longer and Jinny would have snatched her hand away.

Kat had perched on the arm of Helen's chair and was

37

leafing through a magazine, ignoring Jinny. At first Jinny had thought Helen was a young woman but now, with Kat sitting so close to her, Jinny saw that, as usual, Mr. MacKenzie had been right. She was like a puzzle picture, where cubes of black and white flashed into different shapes as you blinked.

At first sight Helen's hair was as blonde as Kat's but, when Jinny looked closely, its perfect colour glinted with a chemical sheen. Flawless make-up flashed to a slackness at her throat; her slim figure couldn't disguise her scrawny elbows; her feet, in sandals almost more miniscule than Kat's, were spread and horny. She was an old boiler. Jinny grinned, remembering Mr. MacKenzie's words and felt Kat's yellow eyes staring at her.

"Lunch, don't you think," twittered Helen. "Jinny must be starving, riding all that way. Next time we must come and collect you."

"There won't be a next time," vowed Jinny silently, as they went in to lunch.

They had melon, served by Mrs. Haddon from Glenbost, who Jinny supposed must be cooking for the Daltons while they were staying at Hawksmoor. Carefully watching Helen, Jinny picked out from the array of cutlery the correct implements for eating melon.

Beside each place were wine glasses. "I suppose they weren't too sure where I'd be sitting," Jinny decided, keeping her eye on the waiting wine glass while Paul crouched over his melon and Helen chirruped.

Mrs. Haddon served the next course. Paul got up, crossed to the sideboard and uncorked a bottle of wine.

"Of course," said Kat, smiling at Jinny with her mouth, "we would all rather have a dry wine, but Paul chose a sweet wine especially for you."

Jinny began to say that he needn't have bothered

because she didn't drink wine, that her father didn't even let Petra drink wine, when she saw Kat's mocking smile.

"She knows I'm going to refuse it," thought Jinny. "She's waiting to laugh at me, make me feel stupid."

A round, convex mirror on the wall sucked the room into its single eye. At this glossy-magazine dining table, amongst these beautiful people, there sat a scruffy girl, tousled hair pushed behind her ears, her face set in a scowl.

Before Jinny had recovered from the shock of seeing herself looking so out of place, Paul had filled her glass.

"And where do you go to school? Do you have to travel miles every day or do you board? Kat goes to boarding school."

"Terston Manor," said Kat as if she expected Jinny to be impressed, but Jinny had never heard of it.

"Inverburgh Comprehensive," Jinny replied. "I ride to Glenbost, leave Shantih there and get a bus in to Inverburgh."

"Oh, quaint," said Kat. She lifted her glass and drank from it, her eyes challenging Jinny.

"Dad will never know," thought Jinny, as she took a mouthful of wine. "It wasn't my fault. I was going to say no, but he didn't give me the chance."

The wine was pleasant tasting, icy cold. Jinny took another mouthful. What she would really have liked was a long drink of limeade, but she supposed the wine would have to do. She tipped her glass up and gulped the wine. Paul refilled her glass. Jinny drained it. Paul refilled it.

"We were sure you would enjoy a sweet wine," said Kat.

Jinny smiled broadly at her. She felt the smile stretched

39

across her face, the corners of her mouth hooked up in a vast grin.

"It's smashing," she said. "Super. Super-duper," and hiccuped loudly.

Kat's laughter seemed to get caught in Jinny's ears, like an irritating fly that would not leave her alone. Jinny shook her head, trying to dislodge it, and glowered across the table at Kat's hazy face. She took another gulp of her wine.

"You'll be one of the locals by now?" asked Helen.

"Goodness no!" exclaimed Jinny loudly. "We've only been here for two years. We used to live in Stopton. Yuk! Was that yukky!"

"Paul has a disco there," said Helen. "Did you go?"

"Me?" said Jinny. "Never."

"Do you like living here?" asked Paul. "Don't you find it rather dull?"

"Finmory is the most wonderful place in the world."

"That's where you live?" asked Paul.

"Finmory House. It's a great big house. The front windows look right down to the sea and at the back it's all moorland. There's a mountain, Finmory Beag. You can climb it easily if you go round the back of it. The view from the top is forever — standing stones, Loch Varrich and miles out to sea."

"All your land?" asked Paul.

"Mr. MacKenzie rents most of it from us," said Jinny, not sure how much of Finmory's land did belong to her father. "But a lot of it is ours."

Paul nodded. His pebble glasses looked like lighthouse lenses to Jinny, dazzlingly bright.

"Is the bay sand or shingle?"

"Oh, sand. Most of the shores round here are rocky bays, but Finmory is sand."

Jinny paused for another mouthful of wine. She had been wrong about the Daltons. They weren't stuck up. They liked her. Even Kat was listening to her.

"How does your father feel, leaving Stopton to come out here?" asked Paul.

"Really," thought Jinny, "he is a most friendly man." She couldn't remember her own father taking such an instant interest in any of her friends.

"I'll tell you this," said Jinny confidentially, leaning across the table towards Paul. "He's a worried man. They've sent his book back. They are not going to publish it."

"I'm not surprised he's worried," said the lips beneath the flashing lenses. "Come to the end of a fairy tale. Thinking about getting back to reality, is he? Nine to five and a pension looking attractive again?"

"Oh no," said Jinny sagely. "He will never leave Finmory. NEVER!"

"How many bedrooms did you say?"

"A lot," stated Jinny. "There are a lot of bedrooms."

Again Kat's laughter was stuck in Jinny's ears. She considered putting her head down on the table but discovered a plate of peaches and cream had appeared at her place.

"Sounds as if you've found what you're looking for," said Helen.

"Yes," said Jinny. "I am always looking for peaches."

Kat's laughter chimed in Jinny's head like unruly bells. With great effort Jinny turned her head and focused on Kat's glinting hair.

"Shut up," she said. "Bloomin' shut up."

Half way through the peaches Jinny couldn't eat any more. She put her spoon down firmly.

"I've finished," she announced. "Absolutely finished."

When Helen gave her black coffee, Jinny took it without mentioning that she always took milk.

"Are you both riding this afternoon?" Helen asked.

It was the very last thing Jinny wanted to do. She felt absolutely terrible.

"We're going to school," said Kat.

"Oh no," exclaimed Jinny. "I'll just watch. Shantih has done enough for today. She wouldn't be fit for tonight if I ride her again now."

"I don't suppose you're fit to ride, either," said Kat, regarding Jinny through slit eyes.

"Perhaps that would be best," said Helen anxiously. "You should have told us that you aren't used to wine. You could have had lemonade."

"Too late now," thought Jinny bitterly. She had made a total and utter fool of herself. She felt sick, a headache throbbed behind her eyes, and she knew that Mrs. Haddon was bound to carry the tale of her behaviour back to Glenbost.

"I'm all right," muttered Jinny, feeling Kat's yellow eyes staring at her.

Half an hour later, Kat, wearing a black jacket, breeches and boots, was mounting Lightning. Her horse was being held by a dark-haired young man whom Jinny recognised as being a farmer's son from one of the neighbouring farms.

"We were so lucky to get Sam Marshall," Helen said, standing beside Jinny, watching Kat. "He's looking after Lightning for us and he can drive the horsebox. He'll drive you over to Miss Tuke's tonight. Mr. Vernon, who owns Hawksmoor, found him for us. So lucky."

Looking at Lightning's gleaming perfection and her

42

shining tack, Jinny had to agree with Helen, but she knew that she wouldn't have wanted someone else looking after Shantih.

Helen and Jinny followed Lightning and Kat down a path until they came to a flat lawn already tracked with a schooling circle.

Jinny collapsed on the grass. She sat staring at Kat, trying to keep her eyes open despite her throbbing headache.

Lightning moved at a balanced, long-striding, extended walk. Kat sat looking like a copy-book illustration of the correct seat. Yet there was something not quite right about her riding. She was too stiff, too perfect, as if she would come off if Lightning shied.

"I expect you'll be looking forward to riding round the cross-country," said Helen kindly, and the thought of Miss Tuke's cross-country obstacles hit Jinny like an engulfing wave. She didn't feel as if she would ever be fit to sit on Shantih again, let alone ride her round a cross-country course.

CHAPTER FOUR

"Magnificent," breathed Miss Tuke, as Kat led Lightning down the ramp of her brand-new horsebox. "That one didn't come from the Horse and Pony Home."

Jinny, still inside the box hanging desperately on to Shantih, wasn't in the least surprised to hear Miss Tuke's praise. She knew Lightning was superb. Standing watching Kat schooling her that afternoon, Jinny had known that Lightning was probably the best horse she had ever seen. She was beautifully schooled, well balanced and smooth in her paces. Kat had ridden her sitting stiffly upright, looking as if someone had bent her into the correct position and perched her on top of Lightning. "Not like me," Jinny had thought. "All over the place. Bet she knows far more than I do — half passes, turns on the forehand and all that sort of thing. Really I don't know anything about riding. I just know Shantih. Bet Kat has had lessons all her life. The best lessons Paul could buy."

"Jinny," roared Miss Tuke. "Move it."

Shantih hovered on the edge of the ramp, gazing down its slope as if she was being asked to descend from the moon.

"It's all right," Jinny assured her. "Go gently. Steady now."

With an outstretched hoof, Shantih tested the insubstantial wood, drew back snorting. Miss Tuke shouted something about all night, and the next second Shantih leapt, tearing the reins from Jinny's hand as she landed far out in the yard to be pounced on by Miss Tuke.

"What an exhibition," sneered Kat, sitting cool and correct on Lightning.

"She is too much for you," warned Miss Tuke, holding Shantih while Jinny mounted. "She'll break your blooming neck for you if you don't pull yourself together."

"Are you really going to ride dressed like that?" Kat asked, as they followed Miss Tuke down to the paddock.

Jinny couldn't be bothered replying. Her headache seemed to have spread in a dull, cold ache all over her. "They can say what they like," she thought. "I don't care. In an hour it will all be over. I'm never, ever riding with Kat Dalton again. Never ever. I don't care if Miss Tuke goes bankrupt."

"We'll do some schooling on the flat first," said Miss Tuke, opening the paddock gate. "Then some jumping."

"Then cross-country," stated Kat. "That is why I am here — to ride over cross-country obstacles. Lightning knows it all, but I've never ridden cross-country. Paul bought Lightning from Alice Moss. She rode her at Badminton. I'm going to ride her in all the big events. That's why Paul bought her for me."

"If whoever you said had won Badminton on her, we would still start with schooling on the flat. How would you feel if you were hauled out of bed and made to jump? Walk on."

"Actually . . ."

"Walk on," boomed Miss Tuke, and Kat did.

Jinny rode round suffering. Dregs of trekkers standing at the gateway gave Shantih the excuse to spook and shy every time she passed it. When Miss Tuke told them to trot, Shantih leapt forward into a canter that turned into a gallop when Jinny fought to steady her. Twice Jinny was carted round the paddock before she could bring Shantih back under control again.

"Don't blame you," Jinny thought, staring down at her hands, not watching as Kat took Lightning round at a collected canter. "You've had a beastly day too. Shut up in a strange stable, shoved into a horsebox and rattled all the way here. You hate it as much as I do. Wish Sue had come and then we wouldn't be here." From Sue, Jinny's mind drifted to Easter. "Wish. Wish. Wish," she thought.

"Right," said Miss Tuke, organising the trekkers to set up three cavalletti poles and a jump of about two feet. "Get your timing right, through the cavalletti, one stride and then over the jump. Round and repeat it."

On both circles Lightning bobbed through the cavalletti, took one exact stride and arched fluid over the pole.

"Knows it all," said Miss Tuke, admiration glowing from her. "She can teach you."

Shantih cleared the cavalletti in one bound and jumped what felt like six feet over the pole. On her second gallop round, she tried to clear the cavalletti and the jump in one leap and landed on the pole with an ominous cracking sound.

"What the dickens has got into you tonight?" demanded Miss Tuke, dragging away the broken pole. "Take her over there and work her at a sitting trot. She'll be jumping over the gate next and smashing it to smithereens."

Jinny took Shantih to a corner of the field, trotted a few desultory circles, then stood watching as Miss Tuke set up different combinations of cavalletti and jumps, making

Kat count Lightning's strides, encouraging her to ride her horse more actively.

Jinny thought about Easter, wondering if Ken had managed to persuade her to eat anything, wondering what Miss Tuke would say when she asked her about the pony.

"One thing for sure, I couldn't have chosen a worse time," Jinny thought, and stared dismally over the hillside dotted with the grazing shapes of trekking ponies.

"We're going out on to the cross-country course," Kat informed her, riding up beside Shantih. "I suppose that will suit you better. At least she won't be able to smash solid obstacles."

Normally a retort would have been blistering Jinny's tongue before Kat had finished speaking, but tonight she had no answer. A leaden weight pulled her down. She turned Shantih, conscious of hand and leg speaking to her horse, conscious of Shantih's stride, her reaching neck, her delicate mouthing on the snaffle. And conscious of the thought of Easter, lying in the field at home with Bramble standing guard over her.

"Of course, as Paul says, mountaineering is the real challenge. He used to climb a lot when he was younger. Still, I think cross-country riding is quite a challenge too."

Jinny had been going to say that with a horse like Lightning that knew it all, nothing was a challenge, but something in Kat's voice stopped her. It couldn't be that Kat was scared. And yet . . .

"We'll ride out to the sheep pen," Miss Tuke said as, riding bareback on a dun pony, she caught up with them. "Take each obstacle as a separate jump. Time enough to be thinking of them as a course."

47

Jinny remembered the sheep pen from the time she had ridden the course in Miss Tuke's cross-country competition. By the time they had reached it, Shantih had been going so fast that Jinny had hardly noticed it. She remembered it only as a neatly timed double.

Tonight when they reached the sheep pen it looked solid and menacing. Once you jumped in you had to jump out. After the sheep pen, flags showed the course sloping downhill over an enormous spread of poles with a ditch on the take-off side. Despite her gloom, Jinny felt her heart lift at the sight of the jumps. A shiver of excitment zigzagged through her. She glanced round at Kat, expecting to see the same brightness answering her, but Kat Dalton's features showed no expression. Her mask was firmly clamped in place. If eyes were gateways to the soul, Kat's were barred and padlocked, allowing no entry to her thoughts.

"Now," said Miss Tuke. "Imagine the sheep pen is in the paddock. Get your stride, timing, and throw your heart over it. No stride in the middle. In and out. Go too fast and they'll be too close to the second part to be able to take off, too slow and they'll stop. Don't let that happen. I do not want to start and take my jump down to let you out. You've got to get it right. Kat, canter Lightning in a circle. When you feel you're ready, another circle, knowing that this time you are going to jump. Then, keeping your rhythm, over you go."

Kat rode Lightning at a steady canter then, increasing her impulsion on her last circle, rode her at the sheep pen. Lightning's ears flicked forward, all her attention on the jump. Her timing perfect, she lifted over the first part of the sheep pen, touched down and sailed effortlessly over

48

the second part. Kat had only sat there. Lightning had done it all.

Jinny watched entranced, half of her filled with delight at the grace of the black mare, half of her tight with jealousy that she should belong to such an arrogant snob as Kat Dalton. Jinny's imagination spun daydreams of how it would have been if Kat had been friendly, for Lightning would have been a perfect pair for Shantih.

"Jinny!"

Miss Tuke's irritation broke through Jinny's dream. She grabbed at Shantih's reins, urging her forward, realising that both Kat and Miss Tuke were waiting for her to jump.

The little bit of attention that Jinny had been paying to Miss Tuke's instruction vanished. Jinny rode Shantih straight at the sheep pen.

"Circle her first! Circle her!"

But it was too late. Shantih, as bored as her rider, snatched at her bit. Head down, she tore at the sheep pen, her torrent of speed scorching the still evening.

"Steady her! Bring her back! Circle her!" roared Miss Tuke.

Jinny was fighting to do just that but there was no time. No time to yell back to Miss Tuke that she was trying to stop Shantih but couldn't. The sheep pen rushed furiously at her. She felt the impact of Shantih's soaring leap connect with her spine, shooting her out of the saddle. Her face was buried in the harshness of Shantih's mane as she glimpsed the second part of the sheep pen beneath her and realised that Shantih was jumping it as a spread. She felt Shantih strain to clear it and then, with drum-beat fury, Shantih was storming downhill back to the paddock.

They raced past a jump of railway sleepers that loomed

49

its barricade frighteningly high, and flew on at the wall. Flags marked where it was to be jumped. Pulling wildly at Shantih's mouth, Jinny managed to steer her between them and over the wall.

Even to Jinny, used to Shantih's speed, they were going at a break-neck gallop, a roller coaster of uncontrollable power where there was nothing else that Jinny could do except hold on.

One more wall lay between Shantih and the paddock but, by the time she reached it, she had raced out of steam. Of her own accord she chose the lowest part to jump, and by the time they were back at the paddock Shantih was trotting, and Jinny, arms and legs chewed string, was back in control again.

"No point in going back up there," Jinny decided. She walked Shantih into the yard, dismounted and gazed ruefully at her blown, muddied horse. The second runaway in one day.

Jinny loosened Shantih's girth, sat down on the edge of a half-empty water trough and waited for Miss Tuke and Kat to come down the hill. She didn't like to think what Miss Tuke would have to say about her performance and she didn't care what Kat said. After this evening Jinny would never see her again.

The Daltons' car swung into the yard, spraying gravel as it skidded to a halt. Paul got out.

"Good evening," he said gruffly. "Where's Kat?"

Jinny looked up the hill and saw Kat and Miss Tuke riding down towards them.

"There," she said, pointing, glad that she wouldn't have to explain why she was sitting there alone.

Paul strode irritably backwards and forwards, turning sharply, digging his heel into the gravel, hands thrust deep into his pockets. When Kat was in earshot he called to her and she came, trotting Lightning into the yard.

"Get in," Paul said, nodding curtly towards the open car door. "We're going out. Helen wants to see you back before we go."

For a second, Jinny could have sworn that Kat's expression changed, her blank mask of sophistication slipped. Whether it was loathing or fear that showed in her eyes, Jinny couldn't be sure, for by the time Kat had sprung down from Lightning her expression was under control again.

"Evening," said Miss Tuke, following Kat into the yard and dropping like a ripe plum from the dun pony. "Some horse you've got there."

"Should be. Paid enough for it. What's the rider like? That's more to the point. Got the guts to ride across country?"

"Did very well," said Miss Tuke.

But Paul Dalton wasn't listening. It was almost as if he hadn't spoken to Miss Tuke, as if his words had been aimed at Kat.

"It's quite a course," said Kat. "Can I come again tomorrow night?"

"If it's not going to be another of your fads that end up with nothing to show for it."

"Tomorrow night?" Kat asked Miss Tuke.

Miss Tuke agreed enthusiastically, and Jinny knew she was thinking about her cash-flow problems. But it didn't matter — it had nothing to do with Jinny.

"Sam will come for you," Kat said, turning to Jinny. "I don't suppose you'll want to risk having lunch with us again."

"I'm not coming. You don't need me."

"Of course I do. It's better for Lightning to be schooled with another horse."

"I can't come tomorrow night. I'm going to Inverburgh tomorrow." It was the first excuse that came into Jinny's head and she supposed it was possible. It was always possible that she might be going into Inverburgh. And she was not riding with Kat Dalton.

From the car, Paul sounded his horn, commanding Kat.

"I will see you tomorrow evening," Kat said to Miss Tuke and ran to the car, her hard hat in her hand, blonde hair rippling. She did not run the way Jinny ran — striding out, elbows eating the air — but as if her breeches were a hobble skirt, her hands with outstretched fingers balanced on air.

Kat got in next to Paul and he revved the engine, fought the steering wheel and drove away without glancing at her.

"Are you going to Inverburgh?" Miss Tuke asked.

"Probably," said Jinny.

"You'll be riding with Kat next time then?"

Knowing that she was just about to ask Miss Tuke for help, Jinny said she might, it depended when Kat was having a lesson.

"Fifteen pounds," said Miss Tuke. "And don't forget I can be doing with it."

"Fifteen pounds for telling me to trot Shantih in circles! Pretty good," Jimmy thought. But she said, "I'm very worried about Easter," and went on to tell Miss Tuke about the pony.

"The trouble is, Dad's not keen on paying any more vet's bills, and I thought if you told him that Easter must have the vet, he would listen to you."

52

"Don't like the sound of it," said Miss Tuke. "She is very old. Well into her thirties. It's a bad sign when they stand about a lot, half sleeping. You can't get her to eat?"

Jinny shook her head, her teeth digging into her lip, fighting to control the tears filling her eyes.

"Tell you what," said Miss Tuke. "I'll come over with you now. Cast my ancient and experienced eye over Easter, then ride Bramble back. I could do with him for tomorrow's trek. Holly's cast a shoe. Ask me, she spends the nights picking them off, the varmit."

"Bramble!" exclaimed Jinny. "Ride Bramble back tonight? But you can't. Easter needs him. Please, please, you can't. What will she do without him to keep her company?" Jinny was back in her nightmare where all safe, secure things would not stay still but changed their shape, grew menacing; she was back where the ground moved.

"What rubbish! She'll have Shantih. It's not as if she'll be left alone," and Miss Tuke marched off to return the dun pony to his trekking colleagues.

"Would you be putting your horse into the box?" asked Sam. "That's her Ladyship's tied up."

Jinny turned blind eyes on him, heard his words but could make no meaning from the noise.

"Here, I'll take her up for you. It's the man she's needing to knock some behaviour into her," and Jinny felt the reins taken from her hand, heard Shantih's hooves skittering on the ramp and Sam shouting at her.

"Not Bramble. Not tonight," beseeched Jinny. "I'll ride him over. Honestly I will."

"I'm coming with you," Miss Tuke shouted up to Sam,

ignoring Jinny. "Room for two of us in there beside you?"

"It is the whole of Glenbost would be fitting in here with me," said Sam, leaning over to open the cabin door for Miss Tuke and Jinny.

"Please don't . . ."

"Now look here, you know perfectly well that Bramble comes back to me in the summer. I never heard such nonsense," snapped Miss Tuke, turning on Jinny. "Get in and be your age."

As they drove back to Finmory, Miss Tuke and Sam talked about the price of hay and the harvest prospects, while Jinny stared straight ahead, willing herself not to cry.

Sam drove to Finmory first. They unloaded Shantih who again sank back on her hocks and cleared the ramp in one leap.

"She is totally out of control," said Miss Tuke, as Jinny led a dancing Shantih down to her field. "Back to her old ways. You wouldn't win anything at Inverburgh Show on her the way she is just now."

Jinny didn't care. She was too worried about Easter.

"Have you stopped schooling her?"

"'Course not."

"If you ask me, all you've been doing is galloping her about. Worst possible thing for a sputnik like her," and Miss Tuke regarded the flaunting Arab with definite distaste.

"I like her the way she is," said Jinny.

"Like her making a fool of you in front of Kat Dalton?"

Jinny didn't answer. The last person she wanted to talk about just now was Kat Dalton.

54

Bramble and Easter were standing together at the far end of the field. Seeing Shantih, Bramble whinnied a welcome but stayed with Easter. Miss Tuke strode across to them while Jinny took off Shantih's tack and set her free to roll.

"Bramble's looking well," said Miss Tuke, as Jinny joined her. "Fat as a pig. A few weeks trekking will soon turn that into muscle."

"Easter?" demanded Jinny urgently.

"You don't need me to tell you. You've only to look at her to know. It's cruelty keeping her alive any longer. She's a walking skeleton. You've done all you can for her. No way is she going to get any better."

"But if I make Dad get the vet?"

"You'll need to get the vet. Tell your father I said so. He'll put her down for you. It's the only thing you can do for her now."

Jinny couldn't trust herself to speak. She wanted to shout at Miss Tuke, telling her that there must be something the vet could do to help Easter. That never, never, would Jinny let Easter be put down.

"I'll hear how it goes," said Miss Tuke, running her broad, short-fingered hand down Easter's neck, resting it for a moment on her bony withers. "It's hard, but the only thing when they reach this stage."

"Let Bramble stay with her."

"Right, my man," said Miss Tuke, grasping Bramble by the forelock. "Trek forward. Remember?" so that Jinny didn't know whether Miss Tuke was ignoring her or really hadn't heard her. "We'll get him tacked up and I'll be off."

Bramble plodded after Miss Tuke. Half-way across the field he turned and whinnied to Easter. Without moving to follow him, Easter lifted up her head and answered him with a high, thin tremble of sound. Bramble plunged to go back to her, but Miss Tuke, hand over his nostrils, elbow in his shoulder, urged him on. "Please couldn't you let him stay? Just till the vet has been?"

"We've all got to work," said Miss Tuke, forcing Bramble on. "I'll be riding him myself until he gets back into the way of things. Expect you'll be wanting him again in the autumn?"

But to Jinny the autumn was too far away to be thought of. The total fear of her nightmare pressed upwards against the edge of her mind. Sheer cliffs of fall lay between Jinny and the autumn.

Jinny held Bramble while Miss Tuke tacked him up and mounted.

"Tell your parents I'll drop in the next time I'm passing. Haven't time tonight."

Jinny stood and watched Bramble being ridden away.

"Really he's mine," she thought. "Mine, and I stand and watch him being ridden away when Easter needs him. If I were Kat, Paul would buy him for me. He would have offered a price that Miss Tuke couldn't refuse, and Bramble could have stayed with Easter."

Jinny went back to Easter, but the pony turned away, didn't want to be bothered with Jinny's attentions.

"I'll get the vet tomorrow," Jinny promised. "He will know some way of helping you. I'll go and ask now."

Jinny walked quickly up to the house. Through the lighted window she could see her parents sitting one on either side of the kitchen table, talking. She could tell from their attitudes that it wasn't the usual evening chat. They were talking about something that mattered.

"Don't care what I'm interrupting," thought Jinny. "I must get the vet for Easter."

She went in through the kitchen door, making a noise so that she wouldn't overhear what her parents were talking about.

"Jinny," said her mother. "How did it go? Did you enjoy yourself?"

Her father glanced up; his elbows were on the table, his fingers interlaced. He twiddled his thumbs, waiting for Jinny to go so he could get on with what he had been saying before she came in.

Her head full of Easter, Jinny could hardly think what her mother was talking about. Her day at Hawksmoor had almost faded from her memory.

"Terrible. Kat Dalton is a stuck-up snob. And I got drunk at lunch. You're bound to hear about it from Mrs. Haddon, so you're better to know now."

"Drunk?" echoed Mrs. Manders incredulously. "How?"

But Jinny wasn't to be side-tracked by such trivial happenings.

"Miss Tuke came back with me. She's taken Bramble away and she says we MUST get the vet for Easter. MUST." Jinny was speaking directly to her father, trying to break through his preoccupation. "It's not just me. It's Miss Tuke says it's urgent. We must get the vet tomorrow."

"Then let Miss Tuke pay for him," said Mr. Manders. "The vet's been and he's told you there's nothing he can do for Easter. She's too old."

"But when he sees her now he may be able to think of something," Jinny insisted. "Honestly, we must get him."

"What's he going to do? Perform a minor miracle? Bring back the dying? And what will he charge for that?"

"Tom," warned Mrs. Manders.

"You MUST get him," said Jinny.

"Money! Money! Money!" roared Mr. Manders. " Do you ever think what it costs to keep Shantih in food and shoes? Never mind Bramble and that old wreck you've installed in the field now."

There was a moment of shocked silence.

"How could you?" gasped Jinny. "How could you say such a thing about Easter?"

"Because I have to pay for it all, that's how."

Jinny and her father stared furiously at each other. Tears welled in Jinny's eyes.

"I hate you," she said. "Hate you."

"Now don't upset yourself. Your father's worried," began Mrs. Manders.

"I don't care what he's worried about. I'm worried about Easter. I've been worrying for days about Easter and not one of you cares. I'll tell you what Miss Tuke said. She said Easter should be shot, and you won't even let me get the vet."

Mr. Manders pushed his splayed fingers through his beard, raised his hands to heaven.

"I have not got the money," he said.

Jinny rubbed eyes and nose on the sleeve of her anorak.

"I'll pay for the vet myself," she said. "I've got pictures Nell has never seen, and when she sees them she'll want to buy them. They're the best I've ever done. And the vet will know how to help Easter. He will. I don't want your money. I'll pay for the vet myself."

Jinny flung herself from the kitchen, diving headlong

for the security of her own room. The phone rang as she passed it. Automatically she picked it up.

"Could I speak to Jinny?" said Kat's voice.

"What?" demanded Jinny.

"We are going into Inverburgh tomorrow. Shall we pick you up about ten?"

"I never. . ." began Jinny, then checked herself. She had been about to tell Kat what she thought about her, to tell her that she never wanted to see her again, when she had thought how much easier it would be if she could get a lift into Inverburgh. Probably the Daltons would bring her home as well. She would be able to phone the vet before lunch.

"Be ready at ten and do wear something a little more respectable than those jeans," and Kat's mocking laughter rang in Jinny's ears.

CHAPTER FIVE

Jinny sat next to Kat in the back of the Daltons' car. They had come for her at ten, and for once Jinny had been ready in time. She had set her alarm for five and when it had gone off she had got up straight away and gone down to the horses. She had said a quick good morning to Shantih, spent a few minutes with Easter who was standing in quietness, her head turned in to the hedge as if she wanted to block out the world, and then come quickly back to her room.

Last night she had taken her folder that held her best drawings out from its hidden place behind the wardrobe, and had just been going to spread her pictures out on the carpet to decide which ones she would take to Nell, when she had heard her father's footsteps on her stair. By the time he knocked on the door, Jinny had the folder hidden again.

"Sorry," her father had said. "Lost my temper. Not at you really. Just everything. They're definitely not taking my book. So money will be less flush than it's been recently. We'll all need to pull our horns in. Okay?"

Behind her hair, Jinny had nodded; had wanted to say she understood about the money being scarce and that of course it didn't matter. They could all live on the vegetables Ken grew and the eggs Mr. MacKenzie gave Mike now that he was more or less working on the farm. Jinny understood about the money.

"Go on," said Mr. Manders, sitting down on the bed

next to Jinny. "Don't bottle it up. Tell me what you're thinking."

"It's what you said about Easter," muttered Jinny.

"About Easter?"

"You called her an old wreck."

"That was only words. I didn't mean to say it."

"You were thinking it," said Jinny, "or the words wouldn't have been there for you to use."

Mr. Manders stretched back his neck, staring at the ceiling.

"You're right," he said eventually, looking back down at Jinny. "But I am sorry I said it. Wish I didn't see her that way. Wish I could see her the way you do."

"I love her," said Jinny.

"Love," said Mr. Manders hopelessly. "Is it too late to send for the vet tonight?"

"Suppose so. It's not really an emergency. But it's all right. You don't need to pay. I'm going into Inverburgh tomorrow with the Daltons to sell my pictures to Nell. I'll pay for the vet myself."

Mr. Manders slapped his palms down on his corduroy-covered knees and stood up.

"If Nell doesn't buy your drawings get the vet all the same. Another ten pounds isn't going to make much difference to the Manders' economy, not with the state it's in at the moment."

When her father had gone, Jinny hadn't felt like sorting out her pictures. She had stood in front of the mural of the Red Horse, staring at it.

The Red Horse plunged from the wall, bursting through the blue-green leaves and white flowers, its yellow eyes blazing. Since Jinny and Keziah, the old tinker woman, had repainted it, the Horse glowed vibrant with colour.

Although the Horse still linked Jinny with the dark, hidden side of herself, she was no longer afraid of it as she had been last summer. Sometimes she would choose not to go into the strange, haunted world of the Horse, would choose to stay in her safe, everyday world, where Petra knew best and doing your homework mattered. But now Jinny saw the Horse more as a messenger of power from that other world; a guide, weird and awe full but a friend as well.

Coming in from Shantih and Easter, Jinny had made a mug of sweet coffee and a peanut-butter sandwich for comfort and taken them up to her room with her. She took the folder from behind the wardrobe, opened it and carefully laid out her best pictures on the floor. They were the very best she had ever done.

"I'll choose four," Jinny had decided and picked up her absolute favourite — a watercolour of Shantih's head with her mane fanned out in the wind. She was about to put it back in the folder when she knew that that wouldn't do. She had to take the best to Nell.

Jinny chose the watercolour of Shantih's head, an ink drawing of Finmory House with her family, their animals and their most prized possessions ranged around it. The third picture was an Indian ink drawing of Bramble standing against a bare hedge in the snow, and the last one Jinny picked was another watercolour of Shantih grazing. Jinny was certain Nell would buy them.

She sat in the Daltons' purring, low-slung car, holding them, carefully wrapped, on her knee. Kat was staring out of the window, Helen chirruping to herself, for no one else in the car was listening to her, while Paul, like Toad in *The Wind in the Willows* was crouched over the wheel. When they reached Inverburgh, Paul bent even closer to the wheel, swearing at other traffic, sweat beading his bald head.

"Now let's see," twittered Helen, when Paul had parked the car. "Paul and I are going to the bank. What have you to do, Jinny? How long will you be?"

"Only one shop," said Jinny. "Nell Storr's craft shop. Shall I come back here when I've finished?"

"Craft shop?" said Helen. "A real craft shop?"

"Oh yes. A super shop. Nell only buys things directly from the people who make them. It's quite different to any other shop."

"Absolutely my thing. Shall we go too?" Helen grabbed Paul's arm, gazing up into his face as if she had been a child begging for sweets.

Paul shook her off irritably.

"After the bank?" pleaded Helen, and Paul grunted, which Helen seemed to take for agreement, clapping her hands and fluttering her eyelashes at Paul.

"Tell us how to get there," she said to Jinny.

"It's not far from here," said Jinny, telling Helen how to reach Nell's and, at the same time, hating the thought of the Daltons getting to know Nell or of them seeing her pictures.

"We'll see you both soon," said Helen, as they all got out of the car.

"Both!" exclaimed Jinny.

"I'm coming with you," said Kat.

"No you're not," said Jinny, horrified at the thought of Kat being there when she was trying to sell her pictures.

"You don't think I want to go with them to the bank, do you? Banks are Paul's drug. He starts getting high whenever he sniffs one and when he's actually speaking to the manager! Wow, is that something!"

"Bye bye," called Helen, twinkling her nail varnish at them as she teetered, high-heeled, in Paul's wake.

"Well, come on then," said Jinny. "But I've something private to talk to Nell about so you'll need to keep out of the way."

"Don't forget we gave you a lift."

"Thanks for reminding me," said Jinny. "Thought I'd flown in on my hang-glider," and before Kat had time to answer, Jinny had dashed across the road just as the lights changed, stopping Kat.

"I expect," said Kat, as she caught up and trotted along beside Jinny's striding walk, "you're wondering about Paul."

"The very last thing I'm wondering about," said Jinny. "So last, I'm not wondering about him at all."

"Why I call him Paul?"

"So what?"

"He's not my father," said Kat. "He's my stepfather. I couldn't call him Dad so I just call him by his first name. He prefers that. And I call Helen, Helen. It makes her feel younger."

"Oh," said Jinny, hardly hearing what Kat was telling her. "Here's Nell's shop."

Nell was standing at the counter wearing a long scarlet skirt and a white top that looked more woven than knitted, with tails of knotted wool and glinting mirror chips. She turned at the sound of the shop door, her ugly, interesting face beneath its afro halo lighting up at the sight of Jinny.

"Ah, Jinny," she said. "I was just hoping some of your clan might drop in."

"Dad's got a load of pots ready for you. Expect he'll be bringing them in next week."

"That is going to be the hard part," said Nell.

Jinny didn't know what she meant, couldn't stop to ask her, for Kat had gone across to the far end of the shop. It was Jinny's chance to show Nell her pictures.

"I know you've not sold all the drawings you bought from me last time," Jinny said, hurriedly unwrapping her pictures. "But I must have some money to pay for the vet for Easter. These are my best pictures, special ones that I was keeping for myself. Please would you buy them. For Easter."

Nell picked up the pictures, holding them with reverence in her heavily ringed hands. She looked at them in silence. When she had seen them all she said, "You would really sell these?"

Jinny nodded.

"Find some other way to make money."

"I need money this morning," stated Jinny. "Please take them."

"They're far too good to sell. And I can't take them. I'm closing down. That's what I wanted to tell your father."

"Closing down?" said Jinny, looking at Nell in blank dismay. "You mean you won't have a shop any more?"

"Been thinking about it for a bit. Sky-high rates. More or less have to be here fifty-two weeks in the year. So I've made up my mind. Closing down. Packing up. Offski."

"But you can't! What will we do without you?"

Ever since they had come to Finmory, Nell had been part of Jinny's life. Someone to be relied on. Someone who was always there. She had bought pictures from Jinny and pottery from Mr. Manders and Ken.

"NO! Oh no!" gasped Jinny. "You can't go."

Another part of the jigsaw that made up Jinny's life had fallen away. No Nell.

65

"But you can't," insisted Jinny desperately, hardly noticing Kat coming across to the counter and picking up her pictures. "You can't go."

"Can," said Nell. "To the Carmargue in France. Blissful place. An old farmhouse. Trite, I suppose, but in the end if it's trite it's right, or, as Iris Murdoch puts it, 'The human heart is ultimately drawn to consolation,'" she quoted. "And I'm getting married."

"Married!"

"To the owner of the farmhouse. You'll meet him at the party on Wednesday night."

Jinny stood small and cold; an alien surrounded by the once familiar delights of Nell's shop that were now so much rubbish — useless bits of wood, clay or stone.

Nell came round the counter and hugged Jinny to her.

"It's right for me to go," she said. "Things have to change."

Conscious of Kat, Jinny wriggled free. "I want things to stay the same," she muttered.

"You'll want then," said Kat, staring yellow-eyed straight at Jinny. "Wanting won't get you anywhere. Are you selling these pictures? I'll buy the one of Shantih's head."

"They're not for sale. Not to you."

"Twenty pounds," said Kat.

"No. I'm not selling them."

"Thirty pounds."

Jinny stared at her in disbelief. "You haven't got thirty pounds."

Kat took three ten pound notes out of her purse and laid them on the counter.

"Thirty pounds," thought Jinny, staring at the notes. "For one picture." She had only to pick up the money and she could phone the vet whenever she got home. He would come to see Easter that afternoon. She wouldn't need to ask her father for money.

Without looking at Nell, Jinny picked up the money. "For Easter," she thought and thrust it deep into her jacket pocket.

"Have you got a bag I could put this in?" Kat asked, as Paul and Helen arrived.

Helen spent two hundred and thirty-six pounds. Paul wrote a cheque. Jinny watched enviously. So much money when her family needed it so badly. For now Nell was closing down, who would buy Mr. Manders' pots?

Nell's party was to be in her flat above her shop. Ken and all the Manders were invited, and by the time they left, Paul, promising a case of whisky, Helen and Kat had managed to get themselves invited too.

"I'll come in and meet your father," Paul said, switching off the car engine in front of Finmory. Mrs. Manders had seen them arriving and came to the door to welcome them in.

Jinny went straight to the phone.

"I sold my picture," she told her father as he passed her in the corridor in answer to his wife's call. "I'm going to phone the vet," and Jinny hesitated, wondering if she should tell her father about Nell closing her shop or wait until the Daltons had gone. Waiting would make it false. It was the kind of news you told someone immediately you saw them.

"Nell's getting married," said Jinny, "and she's closing her shop."

"Oh Lord," said Mr. Manders. "That is it."

"You'll find some other shop. When Nell could sell your

pots, other shops will want to buy them," but Mr. Manders had walked on past Jinny, not listening to her.

The vet's number was engaged and Jinny sat on the stairs, waiting until she could try again.

Her mother and Helen came out into the hall.

"I must admit," her mother was saying, "it was rather overwhelming when I saw it at first. Carpets and curtaining seemed impossible, but we got it together eventually."

"I think it is absolutely gorgeous," enthused Helen. "Not too terribly big. Some of the places Paul buys are mausoleums. I'm only too relieved when he sells them again. We've such a pretty place in Sussex. I couldn't bear to leave it. But something the size of this would be ideal for little breaks."

"As long as you took your little breaks in the summer," clipped Mrs. Manders, so that Jinny knew she didn't think too much of Helen.

"Oh, we'd have central heating installed first thing," smiled back Helen. "If Paul were to buy it, I'd love to decorate it myself."

"You're welcome," said Mrs. Manders.

"Blue, I think," said Helen, half closing her eyes and gazing around. "Powder-blue walls, gold brocade hangings and midnight-blue carpeting. I can just picture it."

"Needn't bother, just picturing it," thought Jinny darkly, as Helen and her mother made their way upstairs.

The third time Jinny tried the vet's number, Jim Rae, the vet, replied. Jinny told him about Easter.

"Miss Tuke phoned me last night. Told me she was pretty done. I'll fit you in this afternoon. Straight after lunch."

"But not to shoot her," Jinny said urgently, knowing what Miss Tuke would have told the vet. "Come and look at her. There must be something you can give her."

"We'll see," said the vet.

"Thank you," said Jinny. "Come down to the field. I'll be there."

Jinny put the phone down and walked quietly towards the front door, intending to go out and down to the field without seeing any of the Daltons again. From the pottery came her father's voice charged with electric excitement.

"But that's an utterly ridiculous price," he said.

"Worth it to me. The minute your little girlie told us about it, I knew it was a more than possible choice. And now I see it, I like it."

"But I tell you, Finmory is not for sale. Absolutely not."

"Dare say you wouldn't mind selling off some of your overheads?"

Mr. Manders laughed. "I'll give them to you."

"There you are. I'm offering to pay you for them. Dare say you got this place dirt cheap, and I'm offering a hundred and fifty thousand plus for it. Think about it."

Jinny stood listening, breath indrawn.

"Definitely not. No question of it," said her father's voice.

Jinny recognised the tone. It was the way she had said No to Kat before she had let her buy the picture of Shantih; before she had picked up the thirty pounds and allowed Kat to take away the painting of Shantih that was the closest Jinny had ever come to capturing the essence of Shantih's being.

Pressing her feet into the receiving floor, Jinny crept to

the front door, cradled the handle in both hands and, easing the door open, went out. She walked down to Easter, blotting out the conversation she had overheard. Never, never, never would her father sell Finmory. Never.

Kat came down to the field looking for Jinny.

"You'll come to Miss Tuke's tomorrow evening?"

"Okay," said Jinny unwillingly, thinking about Miss Tuke's cash flow and the fact that she had gone to the trouble of phoning the vet about Easter.

"I'll send the box round for you. Six o'clock," and the sound of Paul blasting his car horn sent Kat running back to him.

Easter was standing head down, eyelids wrinkled shut, nostrils pulled back. Jinny sat down close beside her, but leaving her alone, not troubling her.

When the vet came he sounded Easter, shaking his head. "Lord now lettest Thou Thy servant depart in peace," he chanted. "Afraid there's nothing else for it."

"I do not want her put down," said Jinny. "You are not to kill her."

Waiting for the vet, she had practised the sentences so that they would come out sounding like statements not like feeble pleadings.

"Why?" said the vet. "What are you keeping her alive for?"

"Just one summer," said Jinny. "That's what I want her to have. There must be something you could try."

"There is something," said the vet. "If you insist."

"Yes," said Jinny.

"Far out chance that it might work," said the vet as he set up his syringe. "It gives a boost to all the organs —

kidneys, liver, heart — but whether she's strong enough to stand it..."

Jinny put a rope halter on Easter and held her while the vet injected her.

"There," he said. "I'll come back, not tomorrow but the next day, some time in the morning. That'll give it time to work if it's going to do her any good. If not I'll have to put her down. It's cruelty keeping her alive in this state."

The vet waited for Jinny's consent, but although she heard him and knew that what he said was true she couldn't speak.

"I'll need someone to hold her for me. Could you do it?"

Hidden by her hair, Jinny nodded, tears pouring down her face.

"That's it then," said the vet.

He clapped Jinny on the shoulder and walked away, leaving Jinny with Easter, holding the halter rope in her hands.

CHAPTER SIX

The next day, immediately after breakfast, Jinny took a feed of oats, bran, chopped apple and carrot down to Easter. She had seen the horses earlier in the morning when she had been on her way to Mr. MacKenzie's for the milk. Shantih, as usual, had come to the gate, eager to welcome her, and although Easter had only turned her head to watch Jinny pass, there had been a brightness in her eye; her ears had been pricked with an interest that Jinny had not seen for days.

"It's working," Jinny had thought. "The injection's going to work." For an instant her old dream of Easter fit again began to build itself up in Jinny's mind. "Stop it," she told herself. "Stop it. Don't go imagining things. It's too soon to tell," and when her family asked her at breakfast how Easter was, Jinny only said, "Much the same," and went on eating her toast.

Now Jinny rattled the feed bucket. "Easter," she called as she climbed over the gate. "Easter. For the pony. A feed for Easter."

Easter looked up at the sound of her name, whinnied, and came towards Jinny. Her bones creaked in their sack of harsh skin, her head was stretched out on its clothes-pole neck, but her eyes were bright, her nostrils quivering. Jinny stood transfixed, hardly able to trust her eyes. It was the first time for days that Easter had shown any interest in food.

"It really is working," Jinny thought. "She really is a bit

better," and chasing off Shantih, she went to meet the pony, talking low, sweet talk to her.

Easter plunged her gaunt head into the bucket, snatching at oats, chomping mouthfuls of the feed, scattering apples, carrots and half-chewed oats in her desperation to eat. Holding the bucket, Jinny couldn't believe her eyes, couldn't believe that Easter could be so much better.

Jinny set the bucket on the ground, ran her hand down Easter's neck and huge-boned withers. She felt a turn of joy deep inside herself. For it was true, Easter was eating, was hungry. Perhaps ... Perhaps ... And for a long moment the dread of tomorrow eased in Jinny's mind. Maybe there was a chance, a chance after all, that Easter wouldn't have to be shot.

Then, as if a switch had been clicked off, Easter stopped eating. She turned away from the bucket, half-chewed food falling unnoticed from her mouth.

"Don't stop," pleaded Jinny. "Eat a bit more. If you eat you'll get strong again. Just a few more mouthfuls. Please, Easter," and Jinny followed the pony, rattling what was left of the feed. "You've only eaten half. You must eat more."

But Easter's eyes closed. She stood still, her head low, and even when Jinny held up handfuls of feed to her mouth she showed no interest, did not even move her head away. Jinny could have been offering food to a wooden rocking horse.

"But she did eat half of it," Jinny kept telling herself as she went back to the house. But no matter how often Jinny told herself that this was true, she knew that there had been something strange about Easter's greed; as if it had taken over Easter, had nothing to do with the pony herself.

"I'll tidy my room," Jinny thought, on the vague

principle that to do something that you really didn't want to do would attract good luck.

"If I do it now, no one will start nagging at me about it," she thought and walked firmly through the hall towards the stairs. She was just about to start the climb to her bedroom when she remembered that a clay model she had made of Bramble should have been biscuit fired by now. "I'll just have a look at it first," Jinny thought. "I'll not glaze it, only look, and then I'll do my bedroom."

The pottery was empty. Jinny walked along the shelves of drying pots, bleaching as they dried from slug grey to brilliant bone, until she found her model. It was a concise statement of Brambleness, solid and self-centred, a nugget of Bramble, weighty in the palm of her hand.

"Now I'm here it wouldn't take long to glaze it and then it could go into the next firing," Jinny decided.

She wandered down to the other end of the pottery. Here her father's desk was littered with papers — invoices, accounts, notes of firing times for different glazes all jostled together. Jinny sat down in his chair and wondered what it would be like to be her father, to have to cope with all the figures that demanded attention, with delivery times that had to be met and accounts that had to be paid. Pushed to a corner of the desk was her father's manuscript still in its shrouds of brown paper wrappings. Jinny tilted back her chair and stared at the paper storm that covered the desk top.

Just in front of her was a typewritten letter. There was a crest printed on the top of the letter, a familiar crest, but for a second Jinny couldn't place it. Then she knew. It was the Stopton coat of arms. It had been at the top of all the official notepaper that her father had used when he had been a probation officer.

A cold clench of fear tightened on Jinny's spine. What

was it doing at Finmory? They had left everything to do with Stopton behind them. Stopton was the past. Her father had left Stopton because he had grown to hate its meanness and dirt; had stopped being a probation officer because he could no longer cope with the stress of being part of a system that trapped people into the squalor of degrading housing, compulsory education that led nowhere; could no longer stand by, watching the rebels being crushed into conformity by legal power.

Because Jinny could read, when her eyes looked at print she couldn't help knowing instantly what the print said.

"Glad you've come to your senses." "Just the job for you." "The interview should be no trouble. Jon Brady is as keen as anyone to have you back." "Rinsed out the Manders coffee tankard." The letter was signed Bill, typewritten beneath the signature — Bill Wright. The Wrights had been friends with Jinny's family when they had lived in Stopton. Bill Wright had worked with Mr. Manders.

Suddenly Jinny realised what she was doing — reading someone else's letter, a letter that certainly wasn't meant for her to see. She sprang guiltily to her feet and dashed upstairs to her room.

She slammed her door shut and stood pressing her back against it. Her whole being was numb with shock, for the letter from Mr. Wright must mean that her father had applied for a job in Stopton.

"To go back to Stopton," thought Jinny in horror. "To do it without telling me, without discussing it with us." Jinny wondered if Ken knew, if Petra knew. Maybe they all knew except her. Maybe for days they had all known; every time they looked at her they had all been thinking, "Jinny doesn't know yet. Doesn't know that we're all going back to Stopton."

"But Shantih," thought Jinny. "What about Shantih?"

The tightness ballooned in Jinny's head and chest. She was back in the Stopton world of unending traffic, roads, city houses, soot-darkened parks and maggot-many hordes of people. No place for Shantih. No free land. Nowhere for Jinny to be.

"Oh no! No!" she cried. "It can't be true. It can't be. We could never leave Finmory. Never."

To leave Finmory would mean that the house would have to be sold. "I'm offering a hundred and fifty thousand plus," treacled Paul Dalton's voice in her head. Did her father mean to sell Finmory to Paul Dalton?

Jinny went back to the pottery to look for her father. She had to find out what was happening.

Mr. Manders was standing by his potter's wheel. A quick glance showed Jinny that the letter she had read was no longer on the desk.

"Is it today the vet's coming back?" Mr. Manders asked.

"For something to say, not because he cares," thought Jinny. "All he's thinking about is going back to Stopton."

"Tomorrow," she replied, and wanted desperately to go on to tell her father she had seen the letter from Mr. Wright.

"He must think there's some hope for Easter or he wouldn't have bothered with the injection."

"I made him try it," said Jinny, and again she searched for words to tell her father that she knew.

"Going over to Miss Tuke's again tonight? Kat seemed pretty full of herself. She was telling us how she is planning to ride at Badminton."

"He's scared of me," thought Jinny in amazement. "He's scared in case I have found out about Stopton, scared in case I ask. Maybe not scared, but not himself, not straight."

"Well," said Mr. Manders, "better get started," and Jinny turned away without having asked what she was desperate, yet terrified, to find out.

Having failed to ask the first time, the second opportunity slipped past more easily. Jinny was washing up the lunch dishes with her mother. There was no one else in the kitchen. She could easily have told her mother that she had seen the letter. But she didn't.

In the afternoon when she was grooming Shantih, Ken stopped to ask about Easter. Jinny didn't mention Stopton. By then it had become something that she didn't dare mention. Perhaps, if no one talked about it, it might go away. Perhaps Jinny might forget that she had ever seen the letter, had ever known anything about it. Maybe she hadn't read it properly, had taken the wrong meaning from it. Jinny didn't think these things clearly, in precise words; somehow they just seeped into her mind and made it seem the best thing to do, not to say anything about Stopton, when really all she wanted to do was to scream at the pitch of her voice, "Why haven't you told me we might be going back to Stopton?"

Her mother had washed and ironed Jinny's anorak, jeans and shirt. Jinny had polished her jodh boots. Regarding herself in the mirror, Jinny decided that on the whole the effect was worse today than her previous appearance had been. Seeing her old clothes carefully laundered, the Daltons would know that they were all she had. Dirty, they had had a certain style about them, and the Daltons must have thought that she was only wearing her old things, her good riding clothes being kept for more important occasions.

Kat had said that Sam would bring the float for Shantih

and Jinny at six o'clock. At half-past five Jinny called good-bye to her family, and yes she had got her hard hat to her mother, and went down to the stable. Earlier in the afternoon she had brought Shantih in, groomed her and cleaned her tack.

Shantih clattered the door of her box with impatient forefeet.

"Get up with you," said Jinny, tacking her up. "Don't know what you're grumbling about. Off for another special lesson." But Shantih was unimpressed. She would rather have been going back to her field.

Since the morning, Easter had refused to eat any more food.

"You're only annoying her," Ken had said when he had seen Jinny holding a cupped handful of oats under Easter's muzzle. "Leave her alone."

And Jinny had had to admit that he was right.

She went out now with a few oats in a bucket, so that they whispered dry and, Jinny hoped, appetizing, against the bucket's sides.

"Easter," Jinny called, crossing the field. "There's a girl. Come on the pony."

Easter turned slowly round and stepped towards Jinny.

"She is going to eat something," Jinny thought, the sudden hope sparking inside her. But even as she thought it, Easter staggered; her front legs buckled and she collapsed to the ground.

Jinny dashed forward and crouched down beside Easter, but now that she was lying down Easter seemed all right, only worn out.

"She hadn't the strength to walk," Jinny thought as she got up and stood looking down at Easter. It was going to happen. Tomorrow the vet would come back and Easter would be killed. "Oh, pony, pony," murmured Jinny, and felt the unavoidable certainty of it choking her.

There was the crashing roar of the horsebox coming up the lane from Mr. MacKenzie's. Jinny ran her hand gently over Easter's neck, over her flat cheek bones, the hollows above her eyes, down the skin-covered bone of her forehead to her dry muzzle. "Oh, Easter, Easter." But there was nothing more she could do. Turning, Jinny left her and went to get Shantih.

Miss Tuke, mounted on a fifteen-hand, overgrown Highland, was waiting for them as Kat's horsebox drew into her yard.

"Action this evening," she called. "We're going for a cross-country ride. Get the gees out and let's get weaving."

"Thank goodness," said Jinny. "At least we're not going to school."

"But I want a lesson," said Kat when they had unloaded their horses. "I need instruction on how to jump cross-country obstacles."

"And that's what you're going to get," said Miss Tuke. "Lightning is going to instruct you."

"Paul's paying you to teach me."

"And I am going to allow Lightning to instruct you on my land. What's more, I'm coming with you."

"That's not ..."

"Jinny, up you get."

Jinny sprang on to Shantih. If she had to ride at Miss Tuke's, this was the best possible riding it could be.

Miss Tuke, followed by Kat and a prancing Shantih, led the way through the paddock and up the hill.

"You'll have heard the old hoary that nothing improves an eventer like a season's hunting?" Miss Tuke asked. "Well, don't think it's cutting up foxes into little bits that improves the nags. It's galloping on, taking jumps as you come to them, loosening up, enjoying yourself."

Jinny could see from Kat's face that she wasn't paying any attention to Miss Tuke. She was staring straight ahead, her lips tight, her black brows drawn together, her fingers gathering up her reins although Lightning was only walking out with her usual calm stride.

"She is nervous," thought Jinny in surprise. "Probably she's not used to riding across country." She smiled at Kat, trying to tell her that it was okay, a bit stomach churning at first if you weren't used to it, but great once you got going; fantastic on a horse like Lightning.

"You've to keep behind Guizer. He knows the way. Jump where I jump. If you think your horse is going to pass me, circle it. You're completely safe as long as you follow me. Right?"

"I should think it's Jinny that you want to warn about not passing you," mocked Kat.

Instantly Jinny wondered why she had bothered trying to be nice to Kat.

"I'm telling both of you," stated Miss Tuke, and she kicked her Highland into a battering trot.

"Easter," thought Jinny. "Leaving Finmory. The impossibility of going back to Stopton. No Nell. The vet tomorrow," and she let the black thoughts stream from her, did not hold on to them as she set herself to follow Guizer's carthorse rump.

They trotted on until Miss Tuke pushed Guizer into a rolling canter. Jinny sat down hard in the saddle, struggling to keep Shantih to a collected canter. Suddenly Miss Tuke twisted to the right, was cantering downhill and over a dry-stone wall. Shantih galloped behind her. Yards before the stone wall she arched into the air, landing far out beyond Miss Tuke on the other side.

"Circle her," yelled Miss Tuke, stopping Guizer.

Jinny hauled on her left rein, swung Shantih round and saw that Kat was stuck on top of the hill.

"Stop holding her back, " yelled Miss Tuke. "Let her come down."

Tight-lipped, Kat held Lightning to a slow trot, clutching at her mane as her horse cat-jumped the wall.

"Terrible," raged Miss Tuke. "There'll be broken bones before tonight's over if you both go on like this. You must not hold her back, Kat. Keep up with us. Frustrate her like that and you'll be in real trouble. Even Lightning won't put up with that sort of treatment."

The make-up stood out from Kat's blood-drained face like a clown's paint. The knuckles on her hands shone through her skin as she clutched her reins. Her lower lip was gripped tightly between her teeth.

"And if you let that idiot career about with you, you'll end up laming her again. Understand?"

Jinny wanted to say that Shantih wasn't used to being kept behind other horses, but she only nodded.

"Great," said Miss Tuke. "Now, next time I'm not stopping. You'll have to sort yourselves out." Guizer, irritated by the delay, shook his storm of black mane, clinked his bit and pounded the peaty soil with his forefeet. "Okay?" and Miss Tuke was away.

Jinny set herself to follow, sat down firmly in the saddle, weighted her feet in the stirrups as she fought to control Shantih. A wall rose from the bracken and Guizer bucketed over it. Shantih stretched and sailed, but Jinny was ready to check her as she landed, to bring her back behind Miss Tuke. Close behind Shantih, Lightning cleared the wall and came back sweetly under control.

But Jinny had no time to pay attention to anything except Shantih. Another dozen strides and Miss Tuke seemed to fall over the edge of the moor as she vanished over a wall with a drop on the landing side. Shantih plunged to follow. Jinny, sitting well back, let her reins slip through her fingers to the buckle, felt her stomach suspended above her as if she were in a dive-bombing lift. Kat screamed. Miss Tuke glanced back, and Jinny knew from her expression that Kat was still on top.

Shantih quickly realised what was happening and understood that if this game of jumping and galloping was to go on she had to follow Guizer, so Jinny was able to sit down and enjoy herself.

Dodging this way and that, swinging her heavy Highland round on his hocks and galloping to left or right, Miss Tuke rode like the Pied Piper over her land. Sometimes the jumps were poles on cans set cunningly in the heather; a brush jump that pounced on them just as they rounded a corner; downhill spurts; walls with wide ditches on the landing side; streams with mired take-offs; and three of the solid cross-country obstacles, which they took without pausing as if they had been no more than the dry-stone walls.

"That shook up the molecules," laughed Miss Tuke, when at last she brought Guizer to a trot and, reins in one hand, turned to look at Jinny and Kat. "There's life in the old bat yet, eh? How did that grab you?"

Jinny was without words, her head a shaken kaleidoscope of images — stone walls flying beneath her, cross-country obstacles held for a fleeting second between Shantih's pricked ears, mud from Guizer's pounding hooves sailing past her face, and the zap of action without thought.

"It was absolutely super," Kat enthused, her voice high with nervous excitement as their mounts walked level with each other again. "It was the most exciting thing I've ever done."

Kat's make-up was no longer perfect, her riding clothes were splashed with mud, but Lightning was her usual calm self, as obedient as ever.

"Wonder what she would be like on Shantih?" Jinny thought. "Wonder if she's always ridden perfectly schooled horses? Wonder how she'd manage if Lightning was really fresh and forgot all her schooling?"

Twice, when Jinny had looked back at Kat, she had been holding on to Lightning's mane, and once, when Lightning had drawn level with Shantih over a wall, Jinny had seen Kat's face puckered with utter terror.

"Oh, it was super. Can we do it again tomorrow night? Jinny, can you come tomorrow?" said Kat, full of enthusiasm now that the ride was safely over.

And Jinny was back drowning in the material world. "Tomorrow" — the word clanged its goblin change. The moors became Stopton's city streets. Where would there be in Stopton for Shantih to gallop and leap? Did Miss Tuke know that they might be leaving Finmory? Had everyone been told except herself?

"Well, even if Jinny can, I can't," said Miss Tuke. "It's the trekkers' film show."

"And the next night is Nell's party," said Kat.

"To say good-bye to Nell," and Jinny thought how much she owed to Nell. Nell had not only said her drawings were good, she had bought them. Say Nell a last good-bye. How she would miss her.

"Couldn't we go over a few more jumps now? Paul won't mind paying."

"It's after eight," said Miss Tuke. "Think of your horse. She's not clockwork. Though from the way she was jumping tonight I wouldn't like to bet on it."

Soon she would be home, Jinny thought. Soon she would be in bed. Soon it would be tomorrow. Tomorrow when the vet was coming back.

"I MUST ride in a real cross-country competition," declared Kat. "Paul would be so pleased if I won something. Couldn't you fix it up? There must be somewhere round about that's holding a cross-country event. Oh, couldn't you?"

"We're hardly in the Home Counties where these things grow on trees," declared Miss Tuke. "But I'll see what I can do for you."

"Cash flow," thought Jinny cynically. "Miss Tuke's fixing will cost you." But she only thought it with the froth of her mind; with all the rest of her being she could only think of Easter, that tomorrow the vet was coming to put her down, to kill her, and he would need someone to hold Easter for him.

"Paul would really be impressed if I rode in a real cross-country event before we go away," Kat went on. That would show that I'm really interested in cross-country. And Lightning could do it, couldn't she?"

CHAPTER SEVEN

Jinny woke early, knowing at once what the day held for her. She sat up, stared out of the window to the horses' field. Shantih was still lying down, Easter standing thrust against the hedge in the far corner of the field. By lunchtime she would be dead. Without calling Shantih, Jinny lay down again. She lay on her back, flat and completely still, waiting. Tears ran out of the corners of her eyes, dripping on to her pillow. Yet in a way, she wasn't crying. She was waiting, tight and hard, somewhere inside herself, knowing that it had to happen. There was no other way, Easter had to be shot. But the tears went on flowing out of her.

Much later she heard Mike getting up and going out to the farm, then her mother.

"It's time," Jinny told herself. The cold, isolated waiting was over. She had to get up now and go down to Easter, stay with her until the vet came.

When Jinny went through the kitchen, her mother was cooking breakfast. The smell of food gagged in Jinny's throat. Slices of dead pig. Slices of dead Easter.

"Morning," said her mother.

Jinny roboted on to the door.

"Where are you off to? Breakfast will be ready in a few minutes."

"Don't want any," said Jinny. "I'm going out."

She had reached the kitchen door.

"It's far too soon to go down to Easter," said her mother. "The vet can't possibly be here yet. Hasn't he a surgery until ten?"

Mr. Manders came into the kitchen, frowsy from sleep, looking for coffee to lure him back to life.

"Far too early," he said, agreeing with his wife. "Have something to eat and I'll come down with you and wait for the vet."

"Perhaps if you'd let me get the vet sooner he wouldn't be coming today to shoot Easter," Jinny said, choosing her words carefully, wanting to hurt her father, saying them because something had to be said between herself and her father. There had to be some noise across the gulf that had opened between them. Really, Jinny wanted to scream at him, demanding to be told what was happening behind her back, why she hadn't been told that they might be going back to Stopton. "Perhaps you should think about that."

Mr. Manders hunched his shoulders, reached for his coffee mug.

"I'll come down when I've had breakfast," he said.

"No," said Jinny. "I don't want you. We don't need you," and she banged the door behind herself.

Jinny walked slowly down to the field. On her way she took a rope halter from the tack room — a rough, knotted halter that Mr. MacKenzie had given to her — and went on to the horses. She spoke to Shantih, watching herself speaking — the film about the skinny, red-haired girl had reached an exciting bit, the cinema audience was sitting on the edge of their seats. As if she sensed the fear in Jinny, Shantih turned away and went to graze in the far corner of the field.

Jinny went over to Easter. The pony didn't even turn her head. She gave no sign that she knew Jinny was there.

Jinny sat down by the hedge and waited. The words, "Thus it is to be an old pony," came into her head. She repeated them over and over again — "to be an old pony". The spell of the words stopped other thoughts from reaching her — the thought of what exactly the vet would do to Easter. Would she groan or scream, rear away from the vet, try with her last energy to escape? Could she bear to hold the halter rope, the hanging rope? "To be an old pony." Even now was there not some way out? Somewhere Jinny could take Easter where they could cure her. If Jinny took her away now and hid her from the vet, perhaps tomorrow she could find someone who could cure her. "Thus it is to be an old pony." The reality of Easter's worn-out body denied all such false hopes. There was nothing Jinny could do except wait. This was real. This was not drawing pictures.

The vet arrived just after eleven. He vaulted over the gate, came striding across the field. Jinny got up to meet him.

"I'm afraid it's no use," he said as he saw Easter. "Well, you've done all you could. Let's get it over with. Poor old lass, you're ready to go, aren't you?"

Easter made a slight movement of her head.

"Not pleasant but it has to be done," said the vet. "Can you put her halter on and we'll take her over to the gate. I'll drop her there. I gave the hunt kennels at Brighill a phone last night. Told them there might be a carcass for them today. They'll come for her this afternoon."

Somehow Jinny fumbled the halter on to Easter, tugged at the rope to try and lead her to the gate. Easter took one step, swayed and stood still again.

"She doesn't want ..." began Jinny, and saw the vet float liquid before her, the grass pound in waves about her head. She heard herself scream, "No!" before the sea of land swept over her.

When Jinny came to, she was sitting on the ground and the vet was holding her head down.

"How's that?" he asked, as Jinny swam back to the sound of his voice and struggled to sit up. "Easy now. Sit still for a minute."

"I'm okay," insisted Jinny and got shakily to her feet. "What happened?"

"You fainted."

"Fainted?" said Jinny, then she saw Easter and remembered what she had to do.

"Nip over and get Jock MacKenzie," the vet told her. "He's used to these things. No point in torturing yourself like this."

Jinny turned and ran. Blinded by tears and hair, she fled across the field, through the gate and towards the track to the farm.

Panic raged in her. No spell of words now to keep her separate. She hadn't been brave enough to see Easter through. Now Mr. MacKenzie would do what she was afraid to do. Would shout and bully Easter to the gate. His hands the last things Easter would know. "But I can't, I can't," cried Jinny.

Ken caught her and held her as she ran full tilt into him.

"Has he shot her?" Ken asked.

"No," sobbed Jinny. "I've to get Mr. MacKenzie to hold her."

"I'll do it," said Ken.

"But you never do. You never have anything to do with killing animals."

"That's why I can hold Easter," said Ken, and he went on down to the field.

Jinny ran through garden and house to her room, threw herself face downwards on her bed and bit hard on her clenched fist. She wanted to stay with her face pressed into her pillow but she couldn't, she had to look.

Through the window she saw Ken standing at Easter's head, his hand on her neck. Saw the vet hold the humane killer to her forehead. Saw Easter crumple and fall. The vet brought a tarpaulin and they covered her body with it.

Even watching from the safety of her room, Jinny felt a flooding sense of relief. It was over. What had to be done had been done. They had reached the other side, and Jinny knew more about herself. She hadn't been able to hold Easter. The courage to have done this was something that she didn't have. Jinny buried her head in her hands and wept.

Ken's footsteps came up Jinny's stairs.

"That's it over," he said. "She was glad to go."

"Thank you."

"I meant to come down before the vet arrived, but Tom caught me. Had something to tell me."

Watching Ken's face, Jinny guessed what her father had told him. She waited, wondering if Ken was going to tell her or if her father had warned him not to mention it.

"So," said Ken, turning to go.

"Wish we could bury her," said Jinny.

"Only a body left. You don't go round worrying what's happened to the clothes you were wearing last year. That's all Easter's left — old clothes."

After lunch, two Hunt servants arrived in a pick-up truck with a crane on it. They fitted a sling to Easter's body and lifted it into the truck. Mr. Manders went down with a bottle of whisky and gave them both a dram. In the late afternoon, when Jinny went down to catch Shantih and ride her, there was only the crushed grass at the gateway and the wheel tracks of the Hunt's pick-up to show that anything had happened. Jinny led Shantih through the gate and the field was empty.

She saddled Shantih and rode down to the beach. Most she wanted to go to bed and sleep, but to go to bed so early would rouse her mother to sympathy or worry and Jinny didn't want either. She let Shantih pick her way over the boulders and then walked her on across the sands. The tide was far out, and Jinny rode Shantih to its frothing, laced edge. She sat staring out at the glittering expanse of sea.

"She's dead," Jinny said aloud. "Easter's dead." Shantih flickered her ears, but Jinny's words meant nothing to her. While the vet had shot Easter, Shantih had gone on grazing. "Like the torturer's horse scratching its innocent behind while his master went about his gainful employment," thought Jinny, remembering a poem by Auden they had read at school. Like the innocent sea that would go on pulsing over the sands when she was back in Stopton. Soon there would be nothing left of Jinny's world. No sign left to tell the strangers that she had been there. No trace. Leaning forward, Jinny threw her arms round Shantih's neck, leant the side of her face against Shantih's shoulder and stared backwards at an upside-down world.

Clattering over the sea-smoothed pebbles, trotting over the sand, came Kat on Lightning. Jinny groaned aloud but she had no will or energy left to escape. She sat and waited.

"They told me I'd find you here," said Kat, bringing Lightning to a halt at Shantih's side.

"Then they were right, weren't they?" said Jinny.

"Your mother said I wasn't to bother you because you were upset. Something about having some ancient old

pony put down. Sounded to me like the only sensible thing
to do. Nothing to make a fuss about."

"Go," said Jinny, "and play in the traffic."

"You won't say that when you hear what I've come to
tell you."

Jinny ignored her, stared out to sea.

"Miss Tuke has fixed it. She's found a riding club that's
having a cross-country event next Saturday, a week
today, and she's fixed it so that we can ride in it."

"Brandoch Riding Club?" asked Jinny, knowing that it
was the only one anywhere near Finmory. "The one
attached to the Country Club?"

"Yes."

"It would be a good idea if you were to ask me what I
want to do before you and Miss Tuke go fixing things. And
anyway she can't have fixed it, the entries had to be in
weeks ago."

"We can't compete against the others but we can ride
the course. 'Hors concour' Miss Tuke called it — she says
it's often done. Paul was delighted when I told him. He
likes competitions. Likes me to win things."

"Then Paul can ride in it if he's so keen. Miss Tuke can
hire out Guizer to him. She can give him lessons."

"Goodness, we are in a tizz-wizz," said Kat. "You don't
really think Paul would ride, do you?"

"Joke," said Jinny. "J. O. K. E. Joke."

"Climbing was his thing."

"You told me. Everest, I expect, when he wasn't so
fat."

"He has climbed in the Himalayas. He was down here
with your father last night having a look at the bay." Kat
clapped her hand to her mouth in exaggerated dismay.
"Hush my mouth," she mocked in a deep-south accent. "I
am not to talk to you about Finmory being sold. You is not

91

to be worried about such things, being too refined in your nature."

Despite herself, Jinny felt her stomach lurch at the thought of Paul Dalton buying Finmory, the thought of the Daltons living in her home.

"They were down here, and your father showed him a rock that hardly anyone has climbed, called the Chimney. That's the kind of challenge that Paul likes."

"That's the entrance to it , beyond the bay," said Jinny, pointing. "You can only see it because the tide's right out."

"Doesn't look anything special to me," said Kat scornfully. "When I was climbing in Wales we tackled far harder things than that."

"Surprise! Surprise!" said Jinny. "You've to go into the cave and look up. It's not just climbing it. It's getting out to it, climbing it and getting back. You can only reach it at very low tide and you've got to climb up and get back before the tide comes in again. A man was drowned in it once. The current at the headland is so strong it would sweep you away if you tried to swim back, and if you're trapped in the Chimney at high tide you've had it. Drowned dead," and Jinny shuddered at the thought. "Dad says it's lunacy. He made Mike promise that he would never try it."

"You are all wrapped up in cotton wool, aren't you," said Kat.

"What is the use," thought Jinny, "of even trying to talk to her."

"Bet Paul could have done it when he was younger. Bet I could do it now. You could ride out, climb it and ride back. Let's go and have a look at it," and although Kat suggested it, her voice was a twanging wire of nervous tension, as if the last thing she wanted to do was to go near the Chimney.

Jinny hesitated. Twice before she had ridden out to the Chimney, once with Mike on Bramble and once with Sue, and she remembered vividly the menace of the black rocks.

"Scared are you?"

"I was checking that the tide was far enough out."

"Couldn't be much further out. Come on," and Kat urged Lightning towards the Chimney.

Still Jinny hesitated. She knew how quickly the tide could turn, how the sea could seem far out one minute and, in no time at all, waves would be pounding up over the sands, the whole bay swallowed up.

Kat turned, shouting at Jinny. Jinny couldn't hear what she said but could see her face mocking, caught her jeering laughter.

"I'll show her," thought Jinny, and cantered Shantih after her. The Arab's hooves splashed fetlock deep, spray rising above her knees. "We mustn't wait," thought Jinny. When she had ridden out with Mike, they had been riding over gleaming sands on their way to the cliffs.

The Chimney was on the far side of Finmory Bay, in the opposite direction from Mr. MacKenzie's farm. It could only be reached from the sands, there was no way of reaching it from above.

"That's it," said Jinny, when they had reached the right place in the black cliffs.

"How do you know? All these cliffs look the same to me."

"Because I do. You go right in there, look up and that's it."

"Here, hold Lightning," and, before Jinny realised what she was intending to do, Kat had jumped down from her horse and handed her reins to Jinny as if she was parking a car.

"In here?" Kat called, splashing her way to the narrow opening in the cliff face.

"Yes, but don't be long. We can't wait."

Kat scrambled over the rocks in front of the cave and ran into darkness. Again Jinny shuddered. There had been no need for her father to make her promise never to try to climb the Chimney. Left to herself, Jinny would never have gone near it.

She looked out to sea, away from the black terror of the cliffs. The tide was coming steadily in. The waves slapped against the cliffs with a changed intention, sending up spumes of volatile lace, brilliant against the ebony backdrop of the rock. Suddenly the far horizon seemed to tip up, threatening to unload tons of ocean on top of Jinny and Shantih.

"Kat! Come on! Hurry up!" Jinny screamed, unable to keep the panic out of her voice.

The minutes that it took Kat to reappear seemed endless to Jinny.

"Come on!" she yelled again. "Hurry up or we're going to be trapped."

Waiting, Jinny thought how it must have been for the man who was drowned here. Had he tried to swim round the cliffs to the bay and been swept out to sea by the current, or had he climbed down from the Chimney to find the waves crashing in on him? Her nightmare stirred in the depths of Jinny's consciousness. She was not thinking about it but it reached her as a rising panic, a nameless fear that made her desperate for action.

"Come on," she screamed as Kat came into sight.

"Calm down," said Kat, deliberately walking slowly towards Jinny, stopping to straighten her jacket before she took Lightning's reins from her. "You're perfectly safe."

Jinny didn't even wait to see Kat mounted. She swung Shantih round and galloped full speed back to the bay.

"The water's not even up to their knees," Kat said as she caught up with Jinny. "Didn't you want to have a look inside? I could climb it without any trouble. Expect I shall if Paul decides to buy Finmory."

Jinny closed her ears to Kat's voice. Even the taunt of Finmory being sold couldn't reach her just now. They had to reach the headland where the cliffs opened into the bay, had to reach it without wasting another second.

"Glory!" exclaimed Kat as they turned into the bay and saw its expanse of sand already shrunk to half the size it had been when they had seen it last. "The tide does come in fast."

"As I did mention," said Jinny, but she was limp with relief. They were safe. For moments before they had reached the end of the cliffs, the swell had been breaking over Shantih's chest. Jinny had felt the grabbing drag of the tide. Five minutes, ten minutes more and they would have had to swim their horses to get round the headland.

"Paul would really be interested in that cave," said Kat, as they walked their horses back through the crimping shallows to the sand. "He would really be impressed if I climbed it."

"What does it matter what Paul thinks? You're always going on about what Paul will think. Do what you want to do."

"You're not allowed to do what you want to do. You're always saying that your father won't let you do things."

"Am not."

"Dare say he won't let you enter for the cross-country in case you hurt yourself."

"He'll say it is up to me."

"Does that mean you're entering?"

"Of course it does," snapped Jinny, caught off her guard.

"I can tell Miss Tuke?"

"Yes."

"You against me?"

"Yes," said Jinny again.

She hadn't in the least meant to get involved with Kat. The last thing she had wanted was a challenge between them. She knew that Miss Tuke thought the course at Brandoch was a stiff one, but it didn't matter. Jinny was sick of listening to Kat's conceit; sick of her boasting, when underneath it all she was so nervous. She would show Kat what Shantih could do. Even if Lightning had cost six thousand pounds that didn't mean to say that, with Kat riding her, she could beat Shantih and Jinny.

"See you at the party," Kat shouted, as she left Jinny to ride back to Hawksmoor.

"Suppose so," said Jinny, wanting to say, "Not if I see you first," and she rode on to the empty field.

CHAPTER EIGHT

Jinny, wearing one of Petra's outgrown dresses, sat on a settee in Nell's room and glowered about her. The party filled Nell's flat with music, laughter and human voices loud in their enjoyment of food, drink and company. It was one in the morning, and the main room of Nell's flat was crammed with dancing couples. Jinny wanted to go home.

"Hate it," thought Jinny. "Hate the smoke and the drinking and the noise; hate Nell going away; hate Easter having to be shot; hate their stupid laughing when there's nothing to laugh about." She wanted to be home in bed with another day safely over when nothing had been said about leaving Finmory.

Ben, the man Nell was to marry, was small with thick, badger-grey hair and an intense, hawk expression.

"Ah, Jinny Manders," he'd said, kissing Jinny, when Nell had introduced them. "I bought one of your drawings, a pencil drawing of an Arab horse. Hangs in my study."

And that had been the high spot of Jinny's evening. The rest had been spent watching her parents' eyes glaze with boredom as Paul and Helen established themselves, one on either side of her father and mother, and proceeded to boom and twitter without pause. Petra had been tracked down by the only young man at the party who was wearing a suit, and Kat was being charmingly sophisticated and so false it made Jinny sick. Mike had stayed at home, and although Ken had come with them he was nowhere to be seen.

"At least try to look pleasant," Petra had said. "You cast such a gloom just sitting there."

"What would you like me to do? Just stand on my head?"

"Oh well, if that's the mood you're in . . ." Petra had said and, abandoning her sister, had gone on dancing with her pinstripe suit.

Even when Nell and Ben had come to sit beside Jinny, inviting her to stay with them next Easter, Jinny had only said she didn't suppose she would and that next spring was too far away to be sure of anything.

"Then think about it later," Ben had said. "Come and dance with me just now."

Jinny had said no, she couldn't, because if she moved about too much in Petra's dress it would probably split.

"In Petra's dress?" asked Nell.

"The one I'm wearing."

"Jinny," said Nell. "Don't."

"Can't help it," said Jinny. "It's the way I feel."

And even when Nell said it had been great knowing her and she would be looking forward to coming to Jinny's first exhibition, Jinny had only been able to make a kind of grunting noise and gone on staring at her feet until they left her alone.

"Nearly two o'clock in the morning," thought Jinny furiously. "Why can't we go home?" And she got up and dragged her way through to the room where the food had been laid out. Only the remains of the feast were left. The cheese straws that Jinny had been hoping for were finished. She stood looking down at the nearly empty plates, wondering if she could eat another chocolate cake.

A door that opened from this room into Nell's studio stood ajar.

"My interview is on Saturday. It's ninety-five per cent certain, but I can't discuss anything definite until then," said her father's voice.

"Don't waste too much time," said Paul Dalton.

"I can't possibly make any decisions until I know I've got the Stopton position."

"Remember, I have my eye on one or two other properties. I want Finmory but..."

Jinny fled back to her settee.

"We're going home," said a girl about an hour later.

Jinny stared at the stranger, not knowing what she meant.

"You've been asleep, haven't you? I told Mum it would all be too much for you," and Jinny knew her sister.

But she hadn't been asleep. She had been sitting, cold and alone, in a desolate, waste world where her own father was planning to sell everything Jinny loved; to take away her home, her own room with the mural of the Red Horse; the sea and the open land; all to be sold without telling Jinny.

She looked up blankly at Petra and wondered if she knew.

"Have you been crying?" Petra asked suspiciously.

Jinny wasn't sure. She shook her head numbly and followed Petra to the room where they had left their jackets. She said good-bye to Nell.

"You will come to see us? Promise?"

Jinny shook her head. It would never happen. Nell had chosen to go and that was that.

Squashed between Ken and Petra, Jinny stared at the back of her father's head as they drove home.

"How could he do it?" she thought. "Knowing how I hated living in Stopton; knowing how I love living here. To have it all fixed up and never to have said a word.

Going for an interview next Saturday and never to have told me. I bet they all know except me."

When they got out of the car, an icy wind was blowing in from the sea.

"Back to winter," gasped Mrs. Manders.

"The ice age cometh," said Ken, as they were blown like dead leaves into the house. "The wolves are running."

Kelly was jubilant at their return, leaping to welcome them back.

"Did you have a good time?" asked Mike.

"Don't tell me you're still up," said his mother.

"Fell asleep in the chair," admitted Mike sheepishly.

"To bed," said Mr. Manders, bolting the front door now that they were all safely home.

Normally it was the moment that Jinny loved — to be home, to know that all her people were securely about her, to be going up to her own room. But tonight there was no security, it was all false. Next weekend, if her father got the job in Stopton, Finmory would be sold.

"Everyone to bed," said Mr. Manders, and began to go upstairs. Mike, yawning, made to follow him. Mrs. Manders was going into the kitchen.

Jinny stood without moving, staring about her, seeing it all with the over-bright garishness of a badly tuned T.V. Suddenly she could bear it no longer.

"No!" she screamed. "No!"

She saw her family swing huge dandelion-clock faces against her. Was sure that they all knew what she was going to say.

"We've got to talk. You've got to tell me, because I know. I saw the letter on Dad's desk about the job, and I heard him talking to Mr. Dalton about it tonight. You can't sell Finmory. You can't. I don't want to go back to Stopton. Why didn't you ask me? Tell me!"

"What's up now?" said Mike. "Who's going back to Stopton?"

"They haven't told you either?" said Jinny. "Next Saturday Dad's going for an interview in Stopton. Mr. Wright's fixed it so that he'll get the job. Then he's selling Finmory to Paul Dalton and he'll turn it into a holiday home."

"Not really?" said Mike incredulously.

"Couldn't it wait till tomorrow morning?" asked Mr. Manders.

"So we could all go on pretending it's not going to happen?" said Jinny.

"I want to know now," said Mike.

Mrs. Manders made coffee, they opened up the Aga and sat round the kitchen table.

"We didn't want to upset you," Mrs. Manders said. "You were so worried about Easter. And when you would insist on seeing the whole thing through yourself, it seemed so unfair to burden you with this as well."

"But how could you think it would help me, not telling me?"

"It may not happen," said Mr. Manders.

"Then you would never have told me," said Jinny bitterly. "It would always have been there in your minds. Something that Jinny hadn't been told, so that we could never have spoken straight to each other again."

"But what *is* happening?" demanded Mike. "You never told me either."

"Ken knew and I knew," said Petra. "Mum and Dad knew I'd be sensible about it. Not start and make a scene."

"We just have not got enough money to go on living here," said Mr. Manders. "Without the income from my writing we cannot afford to live here. I know I should have

101

looked around for other markets for my pottery and not just been satisfied with selling to Nell, and odd batches here and there, but I didn't and there's no use going on about it. And now Nell's gone it's even more impossible."

"But . . ." interrupted Jinny.

"And that is fact," went on Mr. Manders, ignoring Jinny. "To begin with there was still some money left in your grandmother's estate. That's nearly all finished now. When the publisher sent back my book, wanting alterations made in it, I knew I had to do something in case they didn't take it. I wrote to Bill Wright asking if there were any vacancies."

"You couldn't stand Stopton," stormed Jinny. "You utterly hated it. You can't have forgotten how awful it all was. What do you want to go back to that for?"

"Making a scene," said Petra smugly.

"These days you go where there's a chance of a job. They know me in Stopton. Wouldn't have a chance anywhere else. Not at my age. Bill wrote back sending me an application form. They're looking for a liaison officer between the schools and the juvenile courts. Jon Brady would still be my boss. I got on well with him. Wouldn't mind working for him again, so I'm going for an interview on Saturday."

"'The interview should be no trouble,'" quoted Jinny. "I saw the letter from Mr. Wright. I couldn't help reading it. It was on top of your desk."

"So you mean Jin's right. We really might be going back to Stopton?"

"If I get the post, they want me to start as soon as possible. Beginning of September."

"Not go back to school here? But I'm in the football team. I can't leave Finmory."

"And what about Shantih?"

"We won't be going back to live in the city," explained Mrs. Manders. "We'll get a house on the outskirts. Branchford or Wearby. They're both very nice. We'll find somewhere near stables, and you can keep Shantih there. There'll be other children for you to ride with, and you'll be able to join the Pony Club."

Jinny stared blankly at her mother. Here they were, calmly proposing to erupt her whole life, and her mother was holding out the Pony Club as a carrot.

"I never want to leave Finmory," said Jinny. "Never, never. I want to go on living here, keeping Shantih here in her own stable, her own field. I want to have Bramble back again in September, not be going to Stopton. Branchford's all bungalows and Wearby's plastic. I don't want to go and live there."

"Neither do I," stated Mike. "I'm on Jinny's side. And I think you should have discussed it with us before it was all settled."

"But it's not settled," said Mr. Manders.

"Mr. Dalton is going to pay a fantastic price for Finmory," said Petra. "And we can all have a present out of the money. A proper present. I'm to have a new piano, and Jinny can have riding lessons or oil paints or whatever she wants."

"I want to stay here," stated Jinny, not bothering to wipe away the tears that were beginning to trickle down her face, for it seemed as if the whole thing was settled, as if they were already back in Stopton; Finmory no more than a memory, photographs to be shown to people they had known in their Stopton past.

"Wait until Saturday's over," said Mr. Manders. "See if I get the job. Then we'll have a real discussion, thrash the whole thing out."

"Be too late then," said Jinny. "If you get the job, it will have happened."

"Fact," said Ken, speaking from silence, challenging Mr. Manders. "You are fed up living here and, because you want to move, all your family have to go too."

" Not at all. We just cannot afford to stay."

"Rot," said Ken. "And you know it. You have everything here. Put down roots. Grow. Stop being so afraid," and Ken got up, walked long legged to the door, Kelly shadowing his steps, and went out.

"He's right," pleaded Jinny.

"Bed for everyone," said Mrs. Manders. "Half-past three in the morning is no time for discussions."

Jinny went upstairs, sat on her bed with her knees clutched beneath her chin, too desperate even to cry. She could not believe that they really might be leaving Finmory, that her father could possibly think of selling Finmory. She loved it all so much. Knew it as she knew her own being. It was where she belonged. She could never leave it. Yet Jinny knew that if her father decided to go, she would have to go with him. No place for her. She must go where her father chose to go.

She hugged her knees tighter, her shuddering desperation gripped her and shook her. There was no Jinny Manders left, no Shantih, no Finmory. They were all taken by the tempest of the night wind and blown helplessly about the edges of the world.

Then Jinny heard her name called; called without sound from somewhere inside herself and yet, also, from the mural of the Red Horse. Obeying the summons, Jinny crossed her room, went under the arch, drawn to the presence of the Horse. She stood in front of it, seeing it clearly although the room was dark — its powerful being, its unmoving strength, the yellow eyes drawing her to it.

Last summer when Jinny's dreams had been haunted by the presence of the Red Horse, she had experienced it as terror, now she was without fear. She felt the Horse as a source of power, a strength on which she could draw to give her courage. Courage to face what was coming, for the Red Horse offered no easy way out. It did not assure Jinny that they would stay at Finmory; that was in the future. The Horse was NOW and, knowing it, Jinny was drawn out of past, present or future; out of the illusion of time.

Shivering with cold, Jinny came back to herself. The Horse, hardly visible now, was no more than a crude painting. Yet when she lay curled under the bedclothes, on the brink of sleep, Jinny was comforted, her hopeless desperation gone.

CHAPTER NINE

Shantih's neck, with its winnowing mane, arched in front of Jinny as she rode schooling circles at a slow sitting trot. She was concentrating on her riding, forcing Shantih with seat and hands to pay attention to her rider; driving her forward on to her bit; making her use her quarters.

Jinny had woken early, lain thinking about how things were, and at last decided that there was nothing she could do to change them. Easter was dead. Nell's life was her own, Jinny could not tell her what to do. If her father decided to go back to Stopton he would go, and all the family would have to go with him. In a few years' time she would be free to do what she wanted, but now she could only wait to hear the result of his interview on Saturday. It wasn't certain. Someone else might get the job, and then he would come back to Finmory, settle down, forget it had happened. Yet Jinny knew that no matter what the result of the interview was, it had happened. Paul Dalton had offered to buy Finmory, and as long as her father wanted to leave, the threat would be there, and nothing Jinny could do about it.

But there was one thing she could do — she could beat Kat Dalton on Saturday. She would show her that Shantih was better than Lightning; that Shantih could gallop faster, leap higher than Lightning. Even if Kat's horse had cost thousands of pounds and was perfectly schooled, it didn't mean that she was better than Shantih. The desire to beat Kat grew in Jinny's mind until it seemed the most important thing in her life. All the other things were beyond her control, but she could beat Kat on Saturday.

Kat had phoned Jinny that morning, saying in her high-pitched, supercilious voice that Paul, Helen and herself had so much enjoyed Nell's party, and what had been wrong with Jinny that she had sulked all night? They were to go over to Miss Tuke's as usual that evening, and Miss Tuke wanted them to give their horses two hours' road work in the morning, and would they ride together? Jinny had said no, she would see Kat that evening, and hung up.

Jinny knew that Shantih didn't need road work. Shantih was hard and fit, could gallop and leap round the Brandoch course without noticing it. What Shantih needed was schooling. Once she had thought about it, Jinny knew that Miss Tuke had been right. It was months since she had done any serious schooling with Shantih. Now and again she had trotted circles on the sands, but only for a few minutes. Then Shantih would toss her head, kick up her heels saying how bored, bored, bored she was and how about a gallop? Jinny would agree, and off they would go, sea wind blowing against them, the screams of gulls applauding their speed.

Jinny touched Shantih into a canter, felt the moment when she would have leapt into a gallop but was ready for it, caught her in time and steadied her to a collected canter, no faster than a trot. She circled Shantih at the canter, sent her on at an extended canter, brought her back to a collected canter. Then a circle at a sitting trot, then into canter again. She worked for nearly an hour, varying the spells of faster work with figure eights and diagonals at a free and extended walk. Jinny forced Shantih to listen to her, to pay attention, to concentrate.

"You remember it all fine," Jinny told her horse, as she rode a little of the road to Glenbost to comply with Miss

107

Tuke's instructions about a road ride. "Remember to listen to me on Saturday and we'll win okay."

Miss Tuke spent most of their evening lesson schooling over smallish jumps. It wasn't until the end of the lesson that she set up four sizeable jumps made from an assortment of poles and cans.

"Ride the four as a course," Miss Tuke said. "The third's a spread. Let them go on at that. The last's an upright, so you want them back under control before you jump that. Plenty of impulsion. Kat, you go first."

"Thinks we'll smash them up," Jinny whispered to Shantih. "But we'll show her."

"Right, Kat. You'll need to wake her up a bit if you're to clear these."

Lightning had been jumping in her usual calm, fluid arcs. Kat sat in precisely the correct place, bending from the waist as Lightning jumped, her hands sliding forward on either side of her horse's neck. But Jinny couldn't help thinking that there was something wrong about her riding — it was riding by numbers not by the seat of her jodhs. There was no joy in it.

Lightning cleared the first two jumps, and Kat turned her to face the spread.

"Not going nearly fast enough," Jinny thought, as Lightning cantered to the spread with Kat sitting perfectly but doing nothing to encourage her horse.

"Ride her! Ride her!" bawled Miss Tuke, as Lightning put on her brakes, shooting Kat up her neck.

"You must wake her up," warned Miss Tuke, as a white-faced Kat struggled back into the saddle. "Now take her round, and this time let her know that you're intending to jump. Ride her at it."

Kat turned Lightning and rode her clumsily, almost blindly at the spread. The black mare, shaken out of her usual composure, trotted at the jump with a high-kneed, hackney action, her head in the air.

"Canter on. Don't hold her back."

But Kat was clinging on to her reins, shortening them desperately as she approached the jump, all her previous style forgotten.

Lightning cat-jumped, bouncing skywards in a vertical take-off, screwed in mid-air to clear the spread and pitched forward on landing to toss Kat over her shoulder.

"There," exclaimed Miss Tuke catching Lightning. "Told you that would happen. That's what you did up the hill. Hanging on to her back teeth. Up you get and try again."

Kat lay where she had fallen, face into the grass. Miss Tuke crouched down beside her.

"Winded," she said. "That's the way. Lie still for a moment. Get your breath back."

It was long minutes before Kat sat up.

"That's the spirit," encouraged Miss Tuke, helping Kat to her feet. "Up you get again."

"No!" cried Kat, but with a skilled hoist that had reunited many a fallen trekker with her pony, Miss Tuke had Kat back in the saddle.

"Canter round once or twice, then, in your own time, jump the spread and the first two jumps again."

Kat nodded, her face tight, closed in.

"And remember, let her go on at it. She'll take you over if you don't try to stop her."

"She really is scared," decided Jinny, watching as Kat rode round, turned Lightning and, white faced, clutching Lightning's mane, crouched over her withers as the mare stretched to clear the spread. Before Kat could regain control, Lightning rose like a bird over the upright. Letting

109

go of the mane, Kat circled her and she hopped sweetly over the first two fences.

"No problem," said Miss Tuke. "Let her go on over the cross-country on Saturday and she'll take you round it. But leave her mouth alone!"

"Oh, I will," said Kat, loud with relief. "I expect she'll be one of the fastest horses there. I should think if we were competing we would be bound to win."

"Glory!" thought Jinny. "She can't possibly have forgotten that seconds ago she was scared to get on again."

Shantih jumped a clear round. Jinny just managed to catch her when she landed from the spread and stop her doing her uncontrolled tear away over the last jump.

"Could it be," queried Miss Tuke, "that some of us have been doing a little schooling?"

As they walked back to the horsebox, Miss Tuke asked Kat where she had learned to ride.

"We all go to riding lessons from school. Last term Paul discovered that Mark Lawrence's equitation centre was close to school, so I went there to ride. It is absolutely the best place, you know."

"I have heard of it," said Miss Tuke.

"But of course, who hasn't?"

Jinny hadn't but she didn't feel she needed to mention the fact.

"It was Mark who found Lightning for us. Paul wanted to buy me a really good horse so I could compete in top cross-country events, and Mark said Lightning was *the* horse for me. I expect he knew I wouldn't be bothered fighting with crazy squibs that would never be any use anyway."

"She means Shantih," thought Jinny furiously. "There

she is, having flipping well fallen off and been scared to get on and now she's being rude to me again."

"What made you want to take up cross-country?" asked Miss Tuke, before Jinny had time to say anything.

"It was Paul's idea. And mine too. Naturally I've always wanted to ride over cross-country fences."

"Plenty survive without it," said Miss Tuke. "Not like breathing."

"Oh, but I want to," said Kat, almost shouting, her voice saying one thing, her words another.

On Thursday evening they both rode round Miss Tuke's cross-country course.

"Not bad at all," praised Miss Tuke, when Kat had been taken round by Lightning with only one refusal at the spread of railway sleepers, and Jinny had gone clear and in control.

"Well done. The fences at Brandoch won't be any stiffer than those. You will both do very, very well. I shall be proud of you!"

"That will be right," said Jinny, and Miss Tuke said she meant it. It was her new policy of positive thinking.

"No more jumping. Give them a hack tomorrow morning, and you two, plus nags, are coming over here to spend the night. Sam will take the box back to his farm and collect us at seven, at the latest, on Saturday. That means you'll be up at six."

Jinny shivered at the thought of Saturday, not tomorrow but the next day; not only the cross-country but ...

Mr. Manders was going to Stopton on Friday to stay with the Wrights. His interview was on Saturday morning. While Jinny was at Brandoch, Mr. Manders would be answering questions, trying to persuade people that they should employ him, allow him to come back to Stopton. Immediately after his interview he was phoning Finmory to let them know how he had got on. When Jinny came home from the cross-country it would all be settled. If her father had got the job, Jinny knew there was no hope. They would leave Finmory.

Jinny had asked her mother what she felt about leaving Finmory, and Mrs. Manders had replied that it would break her heart but it would be rather nice to live near a supermarket again. Mr. MacKenzie had heard that Paul Dalton had offered to buy Finmory. When Jinny had told him that they might be going back to Stopton, he had spat disgustedly and said the English were "like fleas on a deid dog, aye jumping off." So that Jinny knew he would miss them.

"But it may not happen. It's not definite."

"We'll pick you up at the usual time tomorrow," Kat said, when Jinny had unboxed Shantih and was standing by the Finmory stables waiting for Sam Marshall to drive the box away. "Can't wait to see what you're going to wear for this cross-country."

Mrs. Manders had patched and let out Jinny's original jodhpurs and done her best to clean up Jinny's hacking jacket — letting down the cuffs and moving the buttons. That was what Jinny was going to wear.

"Will it be your jeans?" mocked Kat.

"To tell you the truth," Jinny heard her own voice saying," I'm wearing my new riding clothes. I didn't want to muck them up messing around here but I'll have them on on Saturday."

The box drove away, leaving Jinny transfixed with the awfulness of what she had said.

"How could I? How could I have said that when I know I've no chance of getting new clothes. Jinny Manders, you are an idiot."

"Are you?" said Ken, passing.

"Talking to myself."

"Sign of sanity," said Ken.

"I went and told Kat I had new riding clothes for Saturday. I just went and said it! I'll need to tell her they've been stolen," and Jinny took Shantih into her box.

Ken watched while Jinny watered Shantih and tipped her feed into her trough. The Arab ate slowly, pausing between mouthfuls to gaze into space, savouring the last oat before she took another mouthful.

"Would you like new fancy dress to ride in?" Ken asked.

"Jodhs made from that thick white material," said Jinny longingly. "Black boots, a yellow polo-necked sweater, string gloves with patches between the fingers, and a proper crash cap with an orange silk to tie over it. And, although I wouldn't actually need it for Saturday, I'd love a black jacket," and Jinny twirled around at the thought.

"Light in the darkness?" asked Ken.

"Well ... Light would be having Easter back, fit and well, Nell staying, and Dad seeing how absolutely no one with any sense would dream of leaving here. Oh, but I would love a black jacket."

"I'll buy them for you," said Ken, his slow smile lighting his eyes.

"Don't be daft. You couldn't afford them. Anyway, even if you had that much money I could never let you spend it on riding clothes for me."

"Enough of that," said Ken. "Or I won't. Inverburgh tomorrow morning. Mr. MacKenzie's going in about ten."

"But they would cost hundreds of pounds."

"What do you think I do with the cheque my dear parents send me every month? Tom won't take anything.

113

Even now, when he has this illusion that he is about to be bankrupt, I can't make him take anything. I spend a bit on plants, food for myself, but apart from that I am your supersonic, cheque-book-carrying millionaire."

Jinny laughed aloud at the thought of Ken having a cheque book. "But I couldn't," she said.

"Say that again and you won't get the chance. Do you or do you not want to be all posh-pawed up for Saturday?"

"Oh yes," said Jinny.

"Well then," said Ken.

The thought of boots and a black jacket took Jinny's mind off the sounds of her father packing; helped her to ignore Petra's long messages to be given to Susan Wright by Mr. Manders, which seemed to Jinny to consist of nothing but how great it would be when Petra was living in Stopton again and they would be able to see more of each other.

"How can he want to go back to Stopton?" demanded Mike, punching the cushions of the settee. "I'm not going. I'm staying here. I'll stay with Mr. MacKenzie."

"If Dad goes, we all go," said Jinny. Not long ago she would have been the same as Mike, been making desperate plans to live with Shantih in the stables. But that sort of thing was for books. It didn't happen. For real was Finmory being sold to Paul Dalton. "But it's not certain," Jinny said to Mike, offering him the only hope she had.

"I'm driving in in the morning," Mr. Manders said when he heard that Jinny and Ken were going into Inverburgh. "You can get a lift with me."

"We're going with Mr. MacKenzie," Jinny said, turning her back on her father. "Ken's arranged it."

Ken and Jinny went to the bank first, since Ken felt that shopkeepers might have doubts about accepting his cheques and that cash would save any fuss. It was an old building with a marble floor and marble pillars. Ken danced his way to the counter, a weird, maniac figure surrounded by the respectable citizens of Inverburgh who looked lifeless as sleep-walking zombies compared to Ken's lightness. They were of earth, Ken of air.

"Looks an awful lot," said Jinny, eyeing Ken's wad of notes when they emerged from the bank.

"Give it a passage, set it free," said Ken, and he tore a five pound note into tiny shreds and scattered it, confetti-like, down the wind. "We once burnt a hundred pounds. Great. Like a new element. It set you free."

Jinny, remembering Ken's Stopton friends with their strange eyes, long hair and bright, dangerous clothes, wondered who 'we' had been.

"Morrisons?" asked Ken, naming the exclusive shop that sold everything to do with horses, from pink coats to hoofpicks to made-to-measure dressage saddles.

"There's Bells and Jones," said Jinny. Bells and Jones was a huge store that had a department selling ready-made riding clothes. "It's much cheaper."

"Morrisons it is. The best. That's what money's for. To give us little treats. God takes care of all the rest."

Morrisons' heavy plate-glass door opened on to a paradise of black jackets, breeches, misty-hued tweed jackets, jodhpurs, hard hats stacked on top of each other, rows of boots, and glass counters containing stocks, cravats, ties, gloves, shirts and sweaters. In a side room were saddles and bridles, bits and stirrups and all manner of tack.

A staidly disapproving gentleman took them over to the girls' department and left them with a bright squirrel lady.

"Jinny will tell you what she wants," said Ken and sat astride an old-fashioned, wooden rocking horse to wait.

Half an hour later Jinny emerged from the fitting room.

"Okay?" she asked.

"Pow!" exclaimed Ken. "Boom! Boom! Tremendous."

Jinny was wearing a brown tweed hacking jacket, yellow polo-necked sweater, a crash cap with an orange silk tied over it, cream-coloured jodhpurs, string gloves and black rubber riding boots. She felt stiff and unreal but fantastic. Looking at her reflection in the fitting-room mirror, she had hardly known herself.

"Black jacket?" queried Ken.

"I put the temptation behind me. I need a tweed one."

"Your account, sir," said the squirrel lady discreetly, passing Ken a slip of paper.

Ken took his wad of notes out of his pocket and handed most of it to her.

Jinny wanted to say, "Are you really sure?" but she didn't. She grinned at Ken, lifting up her shoulders, laughing with pleasure. They were super clothes.

"Thanks," she said. "Thanks, thanks, thanks."

When they came out of Morrisons, Jinny clutching her parcels in both arms, there was a man walking along the pavement opposite them. His beard and the hair that ruffed his bald patch were newly shorn. He was carrying his travelling bag over one shoulder, in his other hand was a battered briefcase which Jinny hadn't seen since she'd left Stopton. He was walking smartly, eyes straight ahead. It was Mr. Manders. As they watched, he squared his shoulders and, where Jinny would have flicked back her hair, her father pushed his splayed fingers through his.

"He doesn't want to go!" exclaimed Jinny, knowing the

gesture in her bones, as Mr. Manders walked on without seeing them. "He's forcing himself to go. He doesn't want to go back to Stopton!"

"Let's hope," said Ken, "he finds it out for himself before it's too late."

CHAPTER TEN

The wind began to rise in the early evening, and by the time Jinny and Kat went up to their camp beds in one of the trekkers' bedrooms, the gale was sweeping over the moors, roaring through the pines and raging about the house.

"Don't let it rain," prayed Jinny, waking in the middle of the night, thinking of her new clothes and take-offs churned to mud. Outside, the wind howled like a banshee as it rattled windows, clawed the roof for loose slates and tested the chimney stacks. "Please," murmured Jinny and was asleep again. Next morning it buffeted the high sides of the horsebox as Sam drove them to Brandoch.

"Get that under their tails and we'll see some fun," said Miss Tuke.

"Obvious that she's not riding," thought Jinny. "Or she wouldn't be so cheerful about it."

In the box behind them Shantih and Lightning shifted uneasily. Both horses were excited by the wind. Shantih had refused to box until Miss Tuke attached a long rope to her leather head collar, threaded the rope through a fixed ring at the front of the box and pulled relentlessly, leaving Shantih no alternative but to allow herself to be drawn into the box. Lightning's eyes rolled white-rimmed and her ears zigzagged in frantic semaphore. Between her loosebox and the horsebox she had plunged and shied, flinging herself this way and that in terror at the wind.

"Up to you to give her confidence," Miss Tuke had said, taking the halter rope from Kat and loading Lightning herself. "Day like this you've got to have your wits about you. Seems to be her thing. She can't stand the wind. Still, can't expect her to be totally knitted all the time. Not with her breeding."

"Oh, I love the wind. It makes everything so much more exciting," enthused Kat. "I can't wait to be galloping over the course with the wind blowing all about me."

Kat's hands flickered in wind-blown arabesques to express her words. She smiled at Miss Tuke, her yellow eyes wide, her pink lips laughing, and her make-up as perfect as ever. But her smile was a mask covering up Kat's fear.

Sam had done Lightning for Kat, so that she was as glistening as a show horse, her tack immaculate. Jinny had scrubbed at Shantih's stained knees and hocks, sweated to groom Shantih, her jeans covering her new jodhpurs, her anorak over her yellow polo neck.

It was ten by the time they turned up the drive to Brandoch Country Club. The original stone house was surrounded by snow-cemmed extensions. To the left was a golf course, to the right paddocks hem-stitched with white posts and rails.

Sam followed signs directing horseboxes until they came to an open yard already filling up with trailers and horseboxes. From the cabin window Jinny could see the beginning of the cross-country course — red and white flags horizontal in the wind; a fallen tree trunk that was the first jump; a bulk of telegraph poles stacked solid with straw bales; then steps of two banks to a low pole perched on the edge of the world — over it and you would drop into space.

"Not fair," thought Jinny. "Too soon for a drop like that." You would still be in full view of the watchers at the start. Shantih would hardly have had time to find herself. They would still be horse and rider; separate, not yet fused into one being.

Yet Jinny shivered with anticipation. To ride the course was something positive, something real that she could do, tackle for herself, instead of the interminable waiting — waiting for the results of her father's interview, waiting to be told that they were leaving Finmory for ever.

Jinny looked round at Kat, ready to make some remark about the monstrocity of the telegraph poles, the calculated test of the banks and drop. Kat too had seen the jumps. She was staring out of the window with an expression of numbed horror on her face.

"Coffee?" offered Miss Tuke, producing flasks from a voluminous canvas bag.

"Last thing," said Jinny, and Kat shook her head.

"Green at the gills?" suggested Miss Tuke. "Hours before you have to ride, and we've to walk the course before then. Come on, have a cup. You'll need it."

Jinny wrapped her hands round the hot plastic beaker. Where was her father now? She tried to remember the details of the Stopton Town Hall that she had known so well, but could only picture red-brick walls lichened with soot, pavements pulsing with conveyor-belt crowds and the throb of traffic.

"No! No!" thought Jinny. "Don't let it happen." The idea of leaving Finmory was so impossible that in a way she couldn't really think about it. It was out of thought, pressed down where her nightmare raged. Unthinkable.

"We'll leave the nags in the box," organised Miss Tuke. "You'll keep an eye on them, won't you Sam?"

"Aye, I'll be here."

"And we'll march out and view the enemy."

Before they left the comfort of the cabin, Jinny went into the back of the box to check the horses. They were both electric to the noise of the gale against the sides of the box; rolling eyes glistered white, ears were pinned back. Lightning crashed a peevish hoof against the side of the box and strained her neck against the halter rope. Jinny held Shantih's head between her hands, smooched her face against the soft muzzle. "Win," she whispered. "We're going to beat Kat. We are."

"Bedding down for the day?" called Miss Tuke.

"They're okay," said Jinny, returning. "But I'll need plenty of time to ride Shantih in."

"Come on then," said Miss Tuke.

They jumped down from the cabin into a raging world. The wind bannered out Jinny's hair, ballooned Miss Tuke's unzipped nylon jacket, and blew Kat's silk headscarf over her face as they made their way to where the secretary was installed in a trailer.

Horses and ponies were already being ridden in. All were high with the wind. Their riders' voices, shouting against them, were cultivated with long-drawn-out vowel sounds, but all, or so it seemed to Jinny, held a note of nervous tension. When they had entered for the cross-country they had imagined a calm summer day, not this fury of the wind spirits.

Miss Tuke knew the secretary.

"Sophie!" she cried, beaming on the hook-nosed, scarlet-cheeked woman. "What a day you've picked."

"Chaos, utter chaos. Waiting to hear that some of the fences are on the move, but at least it's not raining."

"Do appreciate you fitting these two in. Both frightfully keen to have a jolly round."

"In Class Two, Junior Twelve to Sixteen Years of Age?" asked the secretary, shuffling papers.

There were three classes. Junior Under Twelve Years of Age, which was over a different course and had already started; Junior Twelve to Sixteen Years of Age, which was over a modified section of the permanent cross-country course; and Senior, over the full course.

"We've had a last-minute cancellation," said the secretary. "Would one of you take his place? It will be Number Ten. Normally we stick hors concours people — the ones who're not competing — on at the end, but it would help us keep things straight if one of you slotted in there."

"Certainly," said Miss Tuke. "Kat?"

"Oh no," said Kat swiftly. "Paul and Helen are coming to watch. I don't want to ride before they get here."

Jinny took the Number Ten tabard. Kat, the last to ride, was Number Sixteen.

They stopped outside to study the plan of the course pinned to the trailer's side, but the carefully inked tracks meant nothing to Jinny. On the plan, the banks and drop, so huge in reality, were inoffensive lines, held no relation to the solid obstacles that Jinny could see if she turned her head.

Kat asked questions about take-offs and angles of approach, tracing out the course with a well-manicured finger, putting off actually seeing the fences.

"Let's get weaving," said Miss Tuke. "I can explain things as we go round."

"Now, in our class we don't jump the whole course, do we?" questioned Kat. "Is that the bit we miss out?"

"That's it," said Miss Tuke impatiently. "It'll be clearly marked. Come on," and she strode out to the start, her green wellies marching her on as if she were a wound-up clockwork toy.

"It is such a wind," Kat said to Jinny. "Wouldn't you think they'd cancel it on a day like this? No horse could jump at its best on a day like this."

"If it was the second flood," said Jinny, "they'd fit it in before the water got too deep."

"I'm really lucky getting a chance like this. I was saying to Paul last night what a piece of luck it was fitting this in while we're staying at Hawksmoor."

"Straight forward," said Miss Tuke, clapping the fallen tree trunk that was the first obstacle.

"We'll clear that okay," squeaked Kat, her voice strained and high. "Lightning won't even know it's there."

"Fair spread over the telegraph poles. The straw bales make it quite a jump. You'll need to have them going on from the start. Not out of control, Miss Manders, but a good going canter. Try holding Lightning back and you've had it Kat."

"I shan't hold her back. Time counts, doesn't it? Why would I want to hold her back?"

Jinny thought Miss Tuke was going to tell her why, but she checked herself and stood, hands on hips, viewing the third jump.

"It's a bouncer," said Miss Tuke. "Up, up, over and drop. Too long a stride and they'll try to take both steps in one, and then you're in trouble for the drop. Steady control. Ride straight at it and they'll take you over."

"Thank goodness there's a decent jump that can be seen from the start," said Kat. "Paul should get some idea of how good Lightning is when he sees me take her over those two."

"Puke and double puke," thought Jinny.

On the far side of the drop, the land dipped then rose again to give a level run-in to a low white gate. Once over the gate, they had left the field behind them and were into woodland. The track wound through trees, the going treacherous with roots and slippery with fallen leaves.

"Take a breather here. I don't mean have a picnic, but let them settle into their canter. You're not here to win. You're only aim is to get round."

"I'm here to win," thought Jinny. "To beat Kat."

"Oh, but Paul expects me to win. He always . . ."

Jinny stopped listening; she was thinking about her father, knowing that his interview might be over. Already he might have phoned home. Her mother, Petra and Mike might know if he had got the job. The pit of leaving Finmory opened at her feet.

She plodded on, vaguely aware of impossibly high jumps — poles into a dew pond, barrels to be jumped downhill, wattles lashed solidly to a wire fence standing black against the skyline, and a strange 'W' fence that Jinny only thought about after they had passed it. She could see no way of jumping it. She opened her mouth to ask Miss Tuke, but the barrier of Kat's high, nervous, conceited chatter made her close it again without speaking. By the time they reached the fence they would be going so fast that, even if she did know where she intended to take off, it would make little difference to Shantih.

Jinny wondered what Ken would do if they went to Stopton. She didn't think he would stay with them. Go his own way? She had been too afraid of his answer to risk asking him.

"Did you see that, Jinny?" shouted Miss Tuke.

"Yes," said Jinny, not even knowing what she meant.

"Nearly home," encouraged Miss Tuke, as they walked along a lovely stretch of galloping turf then turned sharply to the left across a corner of woodland, over a turfed wall and out again into the fields around the Country Club.

There was another jump of poles and straw, sloped railway sleepers over a ditch, and a last jump of heavy timber posts and rails.

"Well within the scope of both your nags. A walk-over for Lightning."

"She'll wonder why she's being asked to jump such tiny things," said Kat, laughing, but somehow her laughter got stuck, stayed too long on a high note of hysteria.

"If you lose your bearings – red flags on the right, white flags on the left. RED RIGHT. And remember, it is all fun," said Miss Tuke. "Now, who's for the loo before we unbox the horses?"

As they passed their horsebox, Sam leaned from the cabin window, shouting against the wind to tell them that Mr. and Mrs. Dalton had arrived and would see them at the Club.

Paul and Helen were sitting in a corner of the clubhouse, Paul swelling out over a window seat, while Helen perched on a stool opposite him. The table between them was half filled with empty glasses.

"Have a drink," Paul called to Miss Tuke. "Come and sit down. Take the weight off the wellies."

Kat and Jinny had changed in the cloakroom. Jinny had her sweater on, her number over her sweater, her new jodhpurs and boots. All were satisfactorily correct.

"Quick nip," said Miss Tuke, accepting a whisky. "Then we've got to get the gees out."

Paul turned to Kat. Behind his thick lenses his pale blue

eyes were liquid, undefined. With his loose face and blubber lips he appeared a Dr. Who creation.

"Well, did you manage to view the jumps without fainting?"

"It is some course," said Kat. "I can't wait to be riding round it."

"That's my little Olympic gold medallist. You'll show them," mocked Paul, and Jinny saw Helen pick up her glass, tip the clear liquid down her open mouth as if she were swallowing medicine, while Miss Tuke looked up at Paul in sharp surprise.

"You'll let them see how to do it. You're not scared of a few jumps, are you?"

Bright patches burnt on Kat's cheeks.

"Of course I'm not scared," she said coolly and tried to laugh, but the sound was embarrassingly closer to crying than laughing. "Why should I be scared when you bought me such a super horse? Lightning will be the best horse here today."

"Don't need to tell me that. Where do you think the money came from to buy her? Out of the nowhere? Kat, sweetie, grow up. Paul paid for her."

"Who's for drinkie poos?" chirruped Helen, but Paul was not to be diverted.

"I bought her for you because I know you're a winner," Paul continued. "You knew that too, didn't you Miss Tuke? Minute you saw Kat sitting on that horse, you knew she was a future gold medallist? Eh?"

"Oh, Paul, don't," twitched Helen.

"Took her to Mark Lawrence's place. Paid top prices to get her some decent tuition. Oh, beautiful place, everything the best. None of your pony-trekking rubbish there."

Miss Tuke fixed him with a calculating eye, and Jinny could see her doubling her charges for organising Kat's first cross-country ride.

" They brought out a horse for her, magnificent beast. And what happened, Kat? You wouldn't get on it would you? Not your kind of horse. So they bring out this white carthorse, sit her up on it and. . ."

Paul threw back his head, mocking laughter sludging out from between beer-speckled lips.

"You couldn't make it move, could you Kat. Talk about a pea having hysterics on a mountain! Laugh? I nearly ruptured myself."

"Come along, Kat," said Miss Tuke. "You'll show them today," and she stood up.

"Just a minute," insisted Paul. "Let me tell you about her climbing. Sent her on a course to the best climbing instructor I could find. And after three days, back she comes — expelled. With a letter in her pocket asking me to pay for the helicopter they'd had to hire to get her off the rock face. Stuck there screaming, weren't you Kat?"

"Well, that's nothing to be ashamed off," said Jinny loudly. "I wouldn't go climbing for anything. I'm terrified of heights."

"Too much," said Miss Tuke. "Come along, or they'll be calling Jinny's number while we're still pigging it in here."

"See you at the start, darling," called Helen. "What time?"

"About an hour," answered Miss Tuke, hurrying Kat and Jinny out. "Must pop into the loo again," she said. "Sam will help you unload. Be with you in a jiff," and Jinny was left alone with Kat.

There was an awkward silence. Jinny couldn't think what to say when she had just been forced to listen to Kat being humiliated like that.

"He's quite a character, isn't he?" Kat said. "I told you, he is so keen for me to win. Pity your parents couldn't be here today, but then I suppose they'll have other things on their minds. Your dad's to let Paul know tomorrow, hasn't he?"

Jinny hadn't known. Finmory sold. Final decisions to be made when her father came home tomorrow. The clock at the Club doorway said twelve-thirty. If it was correct, Mr. Manders' interview would be over. He would have phoned home. Jinny closed her mind against the thought. She shut out Kat and Paul and everything except the cross-country course and Shantih.

CHAPTER ELEVEN

"Number Ten," called a steward. "You're next," and Jinny rode Shantih towards the start.

The chestnut was tight as a closed spring. Under the saddle, Jinny could feel Shantih's back, hard and resisting, so that she couldn't sit down, was perched where Shantih chose to carry her. Even wearing her martingale, Shantih's neck seemed far too close to Jinny's face. Her new crash cap dug into her ears, and her new boots felt clumsy moon-walkers.

"Steady Shantih, steady," Jinny pleaded, as a force of wind hit them out of the storm, making Shantih surge forward, fighting, mouth braced against the bit for freedom.

Already Jinny's arms and shoulders ached with trying to hold Shantih back. There had been no point in trying to ride her in. Shantih's blood raged wild as the storm. Her clarion whinny rang across the field and, from where Miss Tuke was lungeing Kat, Lightning answered.

"It's only the wind," Miss Tuke had told Kat, as Lightning reared straight up, goggle eyes rolling, nostrils red pitted, mane heraldic, all her schooling forgotten. "Let's get her settled." And Miss Tuke had led Kat away to lunge her in a corner of the field.

Thumb on her stopwatch, the starter looked round for the next competitor.

"For real," thought Jinny. "My first real cross-country. Red on my right," she thought. "Red on my right." For, once past the obstacles she could see, Jinny had no idea of the course.

"Ready? You go on my whistle."

Shantih's forefeet were lances. The power her quarters drove through her body was held in the muscles of her chest, her dancing, violent forelegs and Jinny's hands.

"Three, two, one," counted down the starter. Her whistle was shrill above the wind.

Jinny didn't feel Shantih clear the log, hardly felt her rise over the telegraph poles. Not until they dropped over the pole and came sounding up to the white gate was she really aware of anything. Shantih took off, strides before the gate, and they sailed out into the trees.

"Too fast, too fast," Jinny shouted at her, standing in her stirrups, riding low as a jockey over Shantih's withers, her knuckles braced against Shantih's neck. "Steady. Whoa." At this speed they would only need to touch one of the fixed fences and Shantih would go tail over head, Jinny sprawling into space before she whammed into the ground.

Jinny dug her heels down hard, knees locked to the saddle she fought to establish some control. Furiously Shantih shook her head to free herself from the irritation of the bit; reaching her neck, demanded more rein. In the wood the wind was a chained Titan, tearing the trees down to free itself.

"You'll kill us," muttered Jinny through clenched teeth, knowing that once they were out of the woodland they would be jumping again. Despite her gloves, Jinny felt the reins beginning to slide through her fingers. "Shantih," she cried, and the sound of her own voice burst the bubble of rising fear. She had sounded like Kat.

Jinny grinned, relaxed, began to enjoy herself. She

forgot Miss Tuke's warnings. Shantih's speed was, as it had always been, delight and joy, setting Jinny free.

At the edge of the woodland, the ground sloped down to a stream with a pole beyond it. Shantih cleared both with a reaching leap.

"Red right, red right," chanted Jinny. She was completely lost. Only the visible track, the wind-strained red flags seen out of the corner of her right eye, and the sprinkling of spectators, gave her any idea of where to go.

They were galloping over moorland grass now, over a jump of tyres where Shantih spooked and soared, fearing their crouching, animal shape, then over the wattles lashed to the wire fence. The dew pond rose in spray about them as Shantih flipped over the poles in front of it. The mud caught at her feet. Jinny felt her peck, regain her balance and fight to free herself before she breasted on to firm ground again.

Rising up the next slope, Shantih was still full of galloping but her first fury was dying down. Three strides over the lip of the hill was a row of barrels. Caught off balance, Jinny let the reins slip through her fingers, leaned back in the saddle, her legs stuck forward. She landed on the other side minus a stirrup with her arms wrapped round Shantih's neck, and stayed there until she reached level ground.

Once on the flat she found her stirrup, gathered up loops of rein just in time to see the 'W' jump bearing down on her.

"Jump it! Jump it!" she yelled, driving Shantih at it without the slightest idea of how Shantih could take it. Shantih skidded to a halt, and Jinny saw the two outer bars of the 'W' as a double. "Of course," she shouted. "Stupid girl," and was aware, for the first time, of the jump stewards at the sides of the fences.

Jinny turned Shantih. Keeping her straight between hands and knees, she cantered her at the 'W' again. This time Shantih took off exactly where Jinny wanted her to, so that they bounced neatly, together, through the in and out.

"One refusal," thought Jinny and urged Shantih on. She must have no time faults.

Jinny's eye caught sight of a brush jump to her right, red and white poles crossed in front of it.

"Nearly missed that one," she thought as, just in time, she checked Shantih and swung her round to face the jump. Shantih took one stride and cat jumped. As she galloped on, Jinny half heard someone shouting behind her but it was no concern of hers.

The next fence appeared to be a row of thatched cottages. The front of the jump was painted with windows and doors, the top thatched.

"Don't even remember those," thought Jinny in disgust, as Shantih shot skywards and Jinny clutched mane to stay with her.

At a steady pace, Shantih galloped on through an open gateway and along a broad track between rows of beeches. As far as Jinny could see, there were no spectators. She might have been out for a ride by herself. The beat of Shantih's hoofs, the moan of the wind in the beeches, rose in joy through Jinny's being. The post and rails that barred their way seemed hardly higher than one of her own jumps in Mr. MacKenzie's field. Yet Shantih, of her own accord , steadied herself before she took off, and again Jinny had to clutch at handfuls of mane to stay with her.

The track curved left. Lost in their speed, Jinny vaguely

remembered a stretch of turf she had walked along with Miss Tuke and Kat. She thought she should have reached it by now.

A massive great pile of timber — tree trunks roped together — loomed up in front of them.

"Surely we aren't meant to jump that," thought Jinny. It was the height of a double-decker bus, the height of a house. Monstrous it rushed at them. "Glory. No!" And almost Jinny checked Shantih but stopped herself in time.

She felt Shantih sink down on her quarters, jump from her hocks. Salmon leaping up a weir, Shantih sought upwards. She banked on air to twist herself over the bulk of the timber and poured downward. Crouching over her withers, mane in both hands, feet jammed in the stirrups, Jinny endured. She felt Shantih peck on landing, stagger, so that Jinny thought she must come down, then save herself and gallop on.

Jinny threw her arms round Shantih's neck, shouting her praise. Yet, strangely, there was no one at the timber jump to record her triumph. But it didn't matter, Shantih had cleared it, was Horse.

Checking on her flags, red on her right, Jinny cantered Shantih out of the trees, hopped over a turfed wall and was back into the fields surrounding the Club. The last three jumps seemed nothing compared to the timber pile — more telegraph poles, sloped railway sleepers over a ditch, and a last jump of post and rails flowed beneath them and they were cantering through the finish.

Jinny threw herself from Shantih's back, ran at her side on lally legs that would hardly hold her. As Shantih slowed to a walk, Miss Tuke was beside her.

"Well?" she asked.

Jinny's face shone with sweat and glory. "It was super,"

she said. "Absolutely terrific. Shantih was super. Super. She only stopped once."

"Very good," praised Miss Tuke. "Didn't want to say too much in front of Kat but it wasn't the easiest course. Better get back to her. Almost her turn."

"She'd better watch out for the timber fence," warned Jinny, but Miss Tuke had gone.

"Oh, horse," said Jinny, as Shantih butted her head against her arm. "You were the utter MOST. Dear Shantih. Dear splendiferous horse."

She loosened Shantih's girths, lifted her saddle and began to walk her back to the box to sponge her down as Miss Tuke had told her to do, when she heard Paul Dalton's voice.

"Being led about are we? Feel safer that way, do we? Could have bought you a donkey if you'd let me know sooner."

Paul, with Helen clinging to his arm, was standing close to the start. His voice was carried by the wind as he jeered at Kat.

"We'll wait just a minute," Jinny told Shantih, and walked closer to where Miss Tuke's hand on Lightning's rein prevented her from rearing. "Just to see her start."

Kat, Number Sixteen, was the last to ride.

"Sixteen," called the steward. "Ready to go?"

"Good luck," shouted Jinny. The ecstasy of her ride had wiped her mind clear of anything as petty as beating Kat. "Let her gallop on and you'll easily make it."

Kat turned her head at the sound of Jinny's voice. Her mouth was a hard, set line, her nostrils tight, her flesh drawn in against her bones, her terror visible for all to see.

Miss Tuke released her hold on Lightning's bit ring, and the black horse, wind crazed, reared upright.

134

"She's coming over," thought Jinny in a clench of panic, as Lightning touched down again and Kat rode her to the start.

"Now let's see you blooming win something," yelled Paul. "Don't be nervous, helicopters are standing by, ready to air-lift you over the jumps."

"Three, two, one," shouted the starter, as spectators turned to stare at Paul, drawing away from his disturbance.

Jinny heard the whistle, saw Kat clutch up her reins as Lightning plunged forward. Hardly breaking her stride, Lightning cleared the tree trunk, came at the telegraph poles as if she were a steeplechaser, checked, soared, and landed far out beyond the jump. Kat was a helpless passenger as the black horse thundered to the banks, propped to a halt, then leapt both banks from a standstill. Rag-doll limp, Kat sprawled on air and fell in front of the pole on top of the banks. Lightning refused the drop and rearing round, leapt down and back to the start. Miss Tuke caught her, while spectators and officials crowded round Kat, and Paul's laughter blurted out over them all.

A tweedy mother brought Kat back to Miss Tuke.

"Nasty toss," she said. "But no bones broken. Rather nervous? Not to worry. 'Next time,' I always tell mine. 'There'll always be a next time.'"

Still snorting with laughter, Paul staggered across to them.

"Brilliant! Brilliant! Congratulations," he sneered. "That's the way to do it. This cross-country business is going to be your thing, I can see that. A natural. That's what you are, my dear, a natural disaster," and Paul tipped Kat's chin back, forcing her to look at him as she shrank away.

A bruise was spreading over her left cheekbone, and her

expensive clothes were muddied from her fall. If she had been afraid of riding Lightning, her face, without its usual mask, showed she was equally afraid of Paul as he stepped closer to her, forcing her to retreat. "As usual," said Paul, "you have managed to be outstanding or outfalling. Falling out? Falling off? As always. Oh, most impressive with your big talk before the event, and then this."

"Not here, dear," Helen twittered, plucking at Paul's arm. "Let's go back to the Club. We can see Kat later."

"Sometimes I think you do it on purpose," raged Paul, shaking himself free from Helen. "You do it to show me up. I spend thousands on you, and then this. You enjoy it, don't you? Don't you?"

Jinny stared at Kat and Paul, longing to escape from this involvement that had nothing to do with her, and yet, despite herself, drawn to it. She stood mesmerised.

"'Oh, Paul,'" sneered Paul, mimicking Kat. "'I do want to ride at Badminton. I do, I do. I know I could win.'"

Still Kat cowered in front of him, allowing him to beat her down with his words.

"As if it's a play," Jinny thought. "They both have parts and they've got to stick to them."

"What's the next thing going to be? Back to climbing? Going to tackle the Chimney next, eh? Isn't that what you were telling me last night. 'Oh Paul, I know I could climb the rocks at Finmory. I could. I could. I know I could.'"

Jinny saw Kat's face change, the naked fear that had cried from her was covered up. Her features re-formed, her nostrils relaxed, her lips thickened, her yellow eyes that had been staring at Paul lost their glazed terror and flirted up at him. She lifted off her crash cap and shook out her straight fall of hair.

"Goodness," she said, her voice following Paul's mockery was so similar that, for a second, Jinny hardly realised that it was Kat speaking. "Of course I could climb the Chimney. I know exactly how I would do it. When Lightning's so fast there'd be no danger in it at all. I'd gallop out when the tide was low enough, climb the Chimney and gallop back long before there was any danger of the tide coming back in and trapping me. Of course I could do it."

Kat's words broke the spell that had bound Jinny to Kat and Paul. She jerked back to herself, was aware of Shantih's reins looped over her arm while Shantih grazed about her; of other people staring at Paul, and Miss Tuke still holding Lightning.

"And that is enough of that sort of nonsense," declared Miss Tuke, pulling herself together as Jinny had done. "Let's get Jinny's nag seen to. And you, my lady, are riding Lightning back to the box."

"Of course," said Kat and smiled, gracious, plastic, at Miss Tuke.

"As if nothing had happened," thought Jinny as she led Shantih over to the box.

Jinny and Miss Tuke took off Shantih's saddle and bridle, sponged her down, covered her with Miss Tuke's sweat rug.

"Lead her around for a bit," said Miss Tuke, handing Shantih's rope to Jinny. "She must be fit all right. Don't suppose you dawdled round the course, and she's not much bothered."

"It's because she's an Arab," said Jinny, unable to resist the chance.

Jinny led Shantih through the parked boxes to an empty part of the field, where she walked her up and down.

"That's her," Jinny heard two official-looking ladies say, and then they came cantering across to her.

"Do you know what you did?"

"Did?" demanded Jinny.

"You jumped part of the senior course."

"Those tree trunks?" said Jinny.

"And the cottages and a post and rails."

"They did seem," said Jinny, thinking about it, "a bit higher than the rest of the jumps."

"Afraid you'd be disqualified if you'd been competing, but a pretty good show. Wouldn't mind having that combination in my Pony Club team. Where do you live?"

"Finmory," said Jinny, and realised as she said it, it might no longer be true. "I'm here with Miss Tuke."

"Oh yes. Bit far for rallies. Come back next year, jump the correct course and you'll be the winner."

"There won't be a next year," thought Jinny, drowning in the certainty that her father had got the job, that they were all going back to Stopton.

"No point in hanging about," Miss Tuke said, when Shantih had dried off. "Got to get back. Fix my beadies on the new bunch of trekkers."

Seeing the full haynet, Shantih went willingly into the box to join Lightning.

In the cabin they ate rolls, biscuits and coffee, all provided by Miss Tuke. Then Sam, light foot inside his heavy farmer's boots, shuddered life through the inert mass of the box and drove it away from Brandoch.

Every turn of the box's wheels took Jinny closer to Finmory; closer to the moment when she would walk into the kitchen and know, before her mother spoke, whether they were going to go back to Stopton or not.

Kat's high-pitched descriptions of Paul's discos filled the cabin. Miss Tuke folded her arms, settled her chins and slept. Jinny stared out of the window, filled with the icy knowledge that she was being driven closer and closer to where she would have to listen to the words she dreaded. "He's got the job." Sitting in the cabin, Jinny's feet felt the ground at Finmory's back door, the handle turned in her fingers and she heard her mother's voice.

They dropped Miss Tuke first.

"I doubt if I'll have time for any more lessons," Kat said, "but I do want to thank you for all your trouble. Paul has settled with you, for Jinny and myself?"

"Look here, my lass," said Miss Tuke. "Take my advice. Sell that horse. She's far too good for you. Buy yourself a reliable pony and give up all notion of eventing. It is not for you."

"Goodness," exclaimed Kat. "Because I came off today? Oh, once I get Lightning back to Mark, he'll soon sort things out, and you saw for yourself how keen Paul is for me to do really well. How disappointed he is if I don't."

Miss Tuke put her hand on Kat's shoulder in a clumsy gesture of affection. "Oh well," she said, and shouting good-bye she bustled away.

"I don't suppose we'll see each other again," Kat said, when Jinny was standing outside Finmory stables holding Shantih. "Life will be rather hectic for you, won't it? Packing up and going back to Stopton."

"Thank you for the lessons," said Jinny, because she had never thanked Paul. "And the entry money for today."

"Such a pity Miss Tuke couldn't do more to improve you both. Shantih is such a tearaway."

As Sam craned up the ramp, it blocked out Lightning's sleek face, her twitching ears, sweet muzzle. It was too late for Jinny to say any of the things she had been saving up to say to Kat on their last meeting; to tell her what she thought of her. And anyway, she didn't really feel them now. No longer knew what she felt about Kat.

"Bye," Kat shouted, waving from the cabin window. "Bye. I'll look after Finmory for you. Bye."

"The end," thought Jinny. "Even after today! If I'd let Shantih down the way she let down Lightning I'd have been in the depths for weeks."

But it was all over. Didn't matter any more. She led Shantih into her box, watered her, groomed her, praised her and left her with a feed and a haynet.

"When I come back I'll know."

Slowly Jinny walked left foot, right foot through the garden, across the yard. In minutes it might all be taken from her. The Daltons would live here. Finmory would be theirs.

Jinny opened the kitchen door. Her mother looked up from her ironing and Jinny knew.

"He's got the job," said Mrs. Manders.

CHAPTER TWELVE

Jinny lay flat on her bed, her face buried into the fold of her arm to muffle the sound of her crying. She sobbed her heart out, gulping sobs that rose from the core of her being and shook her whole body with their intensity. She couldn't leave Finmory. Couldn't ever. She loved it too much. She had lived too long in this freedom ever to go back to Stopton. But this was what they were going to do to her, take her back to Stopton. She had grown so used to the open skies, the sweep of the moors and this freedom of sea and sand. All her living was here. Riding Shantih, Jinny had made moorland and bay her own, more so than anyone else in her family. Only Ken in his far walking had shared this kingdom with her. How could she take Shantih to live in a riding school field, to trot along suburban streets, to think a ten minute gallop the most wonderful ride?

"They can't," she wept. "Can't take me away. Can't!" but Jinny knew they would.

Her mother had brought coffee and sandwiches up to her and, sitting on the end of Jinny's bed, had tried to comfort her, promising a family discussion when Mr. Manders came home. Jinny hadn't been able to look at her. She knew her mother's words were false, were only a way of telling Jinny not to make a fuss.

"Please," Jinny had muttered. "Leave me alone. I just want to be by myself. Don't come back tonight. I'm okay. I just don't want to see anyone."

When her mother had gone, Jinny had stood in front of the Red Horse, tears pouring from eyes and nose, her face mottled with crying. But the Red Horse was only a crude painting, without power.

"They'll paint over the Horse," thought Jinny and flung herself back on to her bed, engulfed in hopelessness.

Jinny had no idea how long she had been crying in her room before she remembered that Shantih was still in her box. Jumping guiltily to her feet, Jinny scrubbed at her face with the sodden remains of a box of paper handkerchiefs, changed out of her new jodhs into jeans and sandshoes, pushed her hair back behind her ears and went out to Shantih. No one saw her go through the kitchen or across the garden and down to the stables.

The warm summer evening was toning to grey, the wind that had died down in the late afternoon was rising again. It blew in from the water, whipping back Jinny's hair, lifting white crests on the far line of the sea.

"Late," screamed Shantih, crashing her box door with furious forefeet. "Far too late. Where have you been?"

"Forgot about you," admitted Jinny, reaching for a halter. "Dad's got the job. We're going. Going back to Stopton."

Shantih tossed her head. Her white face was luminous in the gloom, her mane dark flames. She pushed her head impatiently into the halter, charged past Jinny, trying to push first through the box door.

"Ride her down to the bay," said the thought in Jinny's head that was against all the advice that Jinny had ever read on how to treat a cross-country horse after an event. It was the thing that you must never do. But this was Shantih. The time a time of desperation.

Jinny fetched her saddle and bridle, still sticky with sweat, tacked Shantih up and led her out. She sprang into the saddle, sent her cantering along the track to the sea.

Jinny rode through a world that was no longer hers. So

often she had ridden to the bay to lose herself in its immensity of sea and sky, alone on Shantih; felt her human isolation fade away, known herself to be part of the weaving of sea and sky, of gulls and living ocean.

Shantih's hoofs clattered over the bulwark of stones, her ears sharp, her dish face poking eagerly forward. She adventured on.

The tide was far out but coming in fast, and Jinny rode over the sand to the far, iridescent line of the sea. From beyond the sea's horizon the wind drummed up grey cloud kings that rose in ponderous gravity, bowing towards Jinny, arching over her.

This would be the Daltons' bay now. They would be where Jinny was, this view their view, Jinny's kingdom theirs. Tears dried on Jinny's cheeks as they fell.

Suddenly Shantih stiffened, her head shot up, eyes bursting from their sockets she stared out to sea. Her thunderous whinny shook her whole body. Beyond the cliffs to Jinny's left a horse answered, and from behind the rocks came Lightning — reins and halter rope dangling about her knees, her stirrups flying from her saddle. She came charging towards them, through cascades of foam sent up by her plunging hoofs. She came straight up to Shantih, blown nostrils scarlet as she snorted, high-stepping around them, then galloped on. Dark crescents flowed from her hoofs as she high-tailed it over the sand to the boulders and on in the direction of Mr. MacKenzie's farm.

It happened so quickly, was so close to Jinny's dream world that, but for the palpable hoofprints, Jinny might have believed that she had dreamt it all. But the hoofprints were there.

For Lightning to have come galloping from beyond the cliffs could mean only one thing — Kat had ridden her there, ridden her out to the Chimney intending to climb it and ride Lightning back; that somehow Lightning had escaped. Already the tide was too far in for Kat to walk safely back to the bay. She would have to be rescued. Mr. MacKenzie had a boat but he kept it in one of his outhouses, hardly ever used it. Even if he was at home, it would take too long to launch it and row out to Kat. By that time she might have tried to swim back, and Jinny knew that even for a strong swimmer that was impossible, the current at the headland would carry them relentlessly out to sea. If she rode home and tried to phone for help, it would take hours to reach Kat. Jinny had no idea how soon the incoming tide would fill the Chimney, how soon Kat, clinging to the rock, would be swept off and drowned.

There was one chance. It might still be possible to ride Shantih out to the Chimney and rescue Kat. Once she had thought of it, Jinny knew that she would have to do it. If she didn't and Kat was drowned she could never be her true self again. That she might have saved Kat and had chosen not to try would lay death fingers on the rest of her life; would come between her and the paper when she tried to draw; between her and Shantih when she tried to ride.

But fear held Jinny paralysed. The terror of the black rock shivered her spine. Fear of the moment when she could hold on no longer and the sea would suck her down. Fear that through her actions Shantih would be harmed.

"You've got to do it," said the voice in Jinny's head. "Got to. You've no choice. It's Kat's life. Do it now." But she could not force herself to move.

Shantih plunged, wanting to follow Lightning. Released, Jinny turned her to the sea, sent her on towards the cliffs.

Shouting her bannering words of power — "Shantih! Finmory! Keziah!" — into the wind, Jinny galloped through the waves, forcing her horse on, knowing that every moment was vital.

"Maybe I'm wrong," thought Jinny. "Maybe Kat isn't here at all."

As she rounded the headland the water was over Shantih's knees, breaking over her chest. Jinny felt the sucking drag of the undertow. It was far deeper than when she had ridden back from the Chimney with Kat.

"Go on! Go on!" Jinny yelled, forcing her horse on towards the cliffs, and there, standing on the rocks in front of the Chimney, waves crashing about her, was Kat.

"Jinny!"she screamed. " Jinny! How did you know I was here? I thought I'd drown. I thought no one would ever hear me. I thought . . ." and Kat grabbed frantically at Jinny's arm.

Jinny tried to pull Kat up to sit behind her, but Kat's clinging terror tightened on her, dragging her down.

"Spring!" Jinny yelled. "Don't pull at me. Spring up." Shantih plunged away and Kat fell back.

"This time spring when I pull. Now!" Jinny fought to keep a grip on Kat's arm, to stay strong in the saddle, to brace herself against Kat. Sprawling, digging with elbows and toes, Kat squirmed up to cling behind Jinny.

"Saw Lightning," Jinny told her as she swung Shantih round, through the deepening water, to gallop back.

Hauling Kat up had taken longer than Jinny dared to realise. They had almost reached the headland when Jinny felt Shantih lose her footing, surge forward, leaping, springing, thrusting through the water to find it again.

"It's too deep," Jinny yelled, warning Kat. "She'll have to swim. Hold on to me. Hold on!" And with a last, frantic eruption, Shantih was swimming.

Jinny had often swum Shantih in the bay. She knew the moment well, when her horse sank beneath her and the swell of the sea lifted her from the saddle; the moment when she threw her arms round Shantih's neck, twisted her hands into Shantih's mane and half swam, was half carried along, beside her. But that swimming had been in calm seas, under blue, summer skies. Then there had been no limpet Kat.

The shock of the water tore the breath from Jinny as she clung desperately to Shantih. They were no longer carried above the clawing hunger of the sea but had slipped down into it. The horizon was above them. The numbing, icy mass of the water was a living being that slapped and sucked and tore at them with thousands of clawing fingers. The rolling breakers that came riding in, sweeping Shantih off course, were a wolf pack pulling her down.

Shantih's face was close to Jinny's own. It was a face from a Stubbs anatomical drawing, as if some subtle covering had been removed, leaving Shantih's face a peeled death mask, a weird thing, held above the fury of the sea by the unseen mass of her body. Shantih's huge eyes blazed from it like lanterns, burned with silent terror.

Kat, knotted on to Jinny's back, began to scream with a high, piercing hysteria.

"Sing!" Jinny yelled, gulping burning sea water, and she shouted against the waves, "Mine eyes have seen the glory of the coming of the Lord."

She could only remember the one line but it was enough. She shouted it over and over again. It held her to her own centre, stopped Kat's screams from reaching her. For the screaming was part of the sea, part of the force that murmured of sleep, sought to spread them out into a myriad fragments, to lose their identity, to become part of

146

wind and water. To scream was to lose her hold on Shantih and drown.

They rounded the headland to see Finmory Bay a distant curve of sand, the sea filling it. Far beyond them white-crested waves rode in to the shore.

Jinny's hope sank. She had been so certain that once they were in sight of the bay they would be safe, but now she saw the reaching expanse of sea still to be crossed. Shantih too saw the land and renewed her efforts to reach it, giving Jinny new hope.

"Nearly!" Jinny cried. "Nearly there, Shantih. On you go! On you go!" And she felt her horse straining to obey her.

The night was folding in on them, light coming now from the dancing, pulsing face of the water. But soon, soon they must be on firm land again.

"Not long," Jinny cried to Kat. "We're nearly there!" But looking out to the bay, it didn't seem true. Almost it seemed that it was further away. Yet how could that be when Shantih was swimming so strongly towards it?

Forcing her numb body, Jinny looked round, searching for the cliffs of the headland that should be behind them now. When they had been swimming from the Chimney to the headland they had been close to the cliffs, but now the line of the cliffs to Jinny's right seemed to be as far away as the shore and, incredibly, ahead of them. Jinny couldn't think how this could be, for all the time Shantih had been swimming strongly towards land. They were past the headland. They must be closer to land.

And then, with a deadly certainty, she knew. The current that made it impossible for anyone to swim back from the Chimney was carrying them out to sea. Even Shantih wasn't strong enough to swim against it. At the same instant, Jinny felt Shantih tiring, as if her consciousness of their danger had flowed from her to her horse.

"Dead," thought Jinny. "We'll all be dead. All drowned," and Kat began to scream again.

"But it can't be," raged the voice in Jinny's head. "Not us. Not me. I've to go on living for years and years. I've still to paint and draw. Haven't even started. Not me. Not me."

Now that she had realised what was happening, Jinny could feel Shantih being carried further and further from the shore. Jinny's nightmare that had lain dormant for days enveloped her. Was real. Was now. Here was no place to stand. The sea was the evil force that would drag her down, tear her from all she loved. Easter was dead, Jinny had failed to save her; Nell had gone; Finmory taken from her; and Jinny was powerless. There was nothing she could do against it.

Weary now, Shantih was being carried more surely out to sea. The screaming burnt in Jinny's ears as it had in her dream. Its noise carried her away.

But it was not her screaming. She was not screaming. It was Kat that screamed.

"Shut up!" swore Jinny. "Shut your screaming mouth. Shut it!"

And there rose in Jinny a force that said she would not drown. Would not allow her beloved Shantih to drown because of Kat Dalton.

"Go on!" she shouted. "On you go, Shantih, on you go!" And, as if she rode at the timber jump, Jinny gathered herself together for the leap. "No!" she shouted against Kat's screaming. "No!" She would not allow Shantih, her horse of air, to die in an element so foreign to her. It was not right. Not fair.

"Not fair! Not fair!" Jinny shouted through frozen lips,

as if this fairness that she knew in her innermost self was the Law, could not be broken. It was the word of the Red Horse, and Jinny stood before the Horse, felt it come raging from the confines of the wall, burning through the dark, come molten-hoofed over the water.

Shantih raised her head, and the Horse was all about them.

"Not fair to let Shantih drown."

The power of the Horse charged through Shantih. She broke from the current that had drawn her seawards. Jinny felt the incoming tide lift them towards the land. Behind them the sea wolves snarled, fell back defeated.

Wearily, Shantih swam on towards the shore. Jinny's being was ice cold. She could not feel her arms that held her to Shantih; could not feel Kat clinging to her. Could hardly see.

Shantih felt the sea bed under her feet, stood, staggered, pitching forward on aching legs that would hardly hold her. Somehow, grappled on to mane and saddle, Jinny and Kat were dragged towards land. Somehow they reached the shallows and fell on to the sand. They lay where they had fallen, Kat still clutching on to Jinny.

"Home," Jinny thought, fighting off the desire to sleep. "Finmory. Home."

She pulled herself up by Shantih's leg and stirrup, dragging Kat with her. And staggering, falling, sleep walking, they made their way to Shantih's field, where Jinny fought the buckles of saddle and bridle to let the tack fall from her exhausted horse. She threw her arms round Shantih's neck, felt her horse warm, living, vital. By now they might all have been drowned, the living bulk of Shantih sea roiled. "Oh, horse, horse," Jinny sighed.

Arms round each other, Kat and Jinny made their slow way to Finmory. The house was in darkness.

"That you, Jinny?" called her mother's voice.

Jinny went into the hall, clung on to the bannister.

"Yes" she shouted. "I went down to see Shantih."

"Are you all right?"

"Yes. I'm going to have a cup of coffee and then I'm going to bed."

"Don't be long then. It's late," and Jinny heard the bed springs as her mother turned over.

She went upstairs, climbing slowly to her own room. Standing in front of the Red Horse, she felt its power like the sun's energy. She had intended to say some kind of thank you, some acknowledgement that the Horse had saved their lives. But it was not necessary. The power of the Red Horse was in Jinny herself; had always been there, waiting for Jinny to discover it.

Jinny collected bath towels and dry clothes and took them down to Kat. She opened up the Aga, and they changed and tried to warm themselves but couldn't stop chittering — teeth chattering; shaking, shuddering — both knowing they had nearly drowned, so close to being dead, so very close. They had been where there was nothing but flux and flow, no fixed hold, all motion. Had been there and survived.

"I know," Jinny said, and went through to find her father's brandy, poured out two glasses and took them back to Kat. They sipped it, the spirit firing their blood, bringing warmth and life back to sea-cold flesh.

Jinny made bread and butter and heated a tin of tomato soup. They sat over the Aga eating it, not speaking. Thoughts flashed through Jinny's mind and were gone — the moment when the Red Horse had infused Shantih with strength and brought them to the shore; the timber jump; Kat; her father taking the job in Stopton; leaving Finmory;

and even the thought of Finmory being sold flowed through Jinny's mind as the other thoughts had done.

Suddenly Kat began to talk.

"Helen's not my mother either," she said. "My own mother left when I was about five. I can just remember her. We came in from shopping. She put down her basket, it was a wicker basket, on the table and bent over to kiss me, and went. I can remember the smell of her hair. I guess my father was stuck with me. When I was eight, Helen came. She lived with us, looked after me. It was all right. Then my father got tired of her, went off with someone else. This time it was Helen who was stuck with me. We hate each other, but she can't help feeling responsible for me. When she hooked up with Paul, she tagged me along too. I was even their bridesmaid. Suited Paul. He likes his victims to be good looking."

And Kat's voice took Jinny into a world that she hadn't known existed before. A world as terrifying as the maelstrom of sea and wind. Where the rage was the torturous emotions of human beings. Kat told of lying in bed listening to the adults in her life fighting with each other, using her as a weapon against each other; of the extremes of love and hate that had come to seem normal to her; how each day with Helen and Paul was a tight-rope walk of evasion and fear, yet had an addictive compulsion that made ordinary living seem tasteless, no longer enough for Kat.

"I never know when he's going to attack me."

"Not hit you?"

"Might be easier if he did. You heard him today. In a way he made me climb the Chimney. When he finds out that we nearly drowned, he'll enjoy that."

"He won't find out."

"I'll tell him," said Kat, knowing herself. Her wet hair

151

clamped to her head, her thin face without its make-up had no sophistication, was naked and vulnerable. "I want to please him."

"Can't you leave them?" demanded Jinny, sure that she would.

"Where could I go? It's okay when I'm at school. These holidays have been a downer because of Lightning."

"But she's such a super horse. Just ride her, enjoy her. You don't need to jump cross-country jumps. And she is super!"

"I know and so does Paul. He wants to see me getting fond of her. But I won't. He can do what he likes with her. I don't care if he sells her."

Jinny remembered how she had never seen Kat speaking to Lightning, never seen her with her arms round Lightning; only heard her talking about winning to please Paul.

"She's your horse. He couldn't sell her."

"He bought me a dog last summer. I had her all through the holidays. I came back at half term and she'd gone. He said he'd sold her to a laboratory. He was laughing when he told me, so I don't know, do I? Might only have been one of his jokes, but I'll never know."

Jinny had no reply, could not believe such things could happen.

"Paul's the same with people. If he thinks I like them he mucks it all up. So I don't."

"You were so stuck up," said Jinny. "So unfriendly."

"You weren't exactly best friend material yourself. Sitting on Shantih without a nerve in your body, despising us all. And me, scared stiff at the thought of having to jump. Had to cover up somehow."

They grinned at each other. "Might never have known,"

thought Jinny. "So blind I couldn't see the real Kat at all."

"You'll have Finmory," she said, still hardly able to believe it.

"Not a chance. Paul will do it up. Rent it, make money from it. Why does your father want to sell it?"

Jinny shook her head. Suddenly she was too tired to go on talking. Her whole body ached. Against her will, her eyelids dropped leaden over her eyes.

"I called my dog Penny," said Kat, but Jinny was asleep.

When the phone woke her it was morning. Kat's chair was empty. Her wet clothes had gone. The clothes Jinny had lent her lay in their place. Cramped and stiff with sleeping in the chair, Jinny answered the phone.

"It's Kat. I went to look for Lightning. We forgot about her. I found her close to Finmory and thought I might as well ride back here. Less fuss."

"Right," said Jinny.

"Thank Shantih for rescuing me."

"Yes," said Jinny, still dazed.

"And you. Bye."

"Bye."

"And don't worry too much about me. I do enjoy Paul's money, you know," and Kat's laughter mocked in Jinny's ears.

She went back to the kitchen, heard her mother coming downstairs.

"Whatever's happened?" demanded Mrs. Manders, taking in bath towels, dirty dishes, the open Aga and sodden clothes.

"Will tell you," said Jinny, and the outside door opened. Her father came in.

"Caught the night train," he said.

Jinny backed away. It was too sudden. She couldn't face her father just now. Couldn't start to come to terms with the fact of leaving Finmory. Not when she had to sleep. She stared at him suspiciously, warily. That he should have done such a thing.

"Big success?" asked Mrs. Manders.

"We're not going. We're staying here."

"What?" cried Mrs. Manders. "But you said you'd got the job."

"Not going?" yelled Jinny. "Not going?"

"I got the job. All dead keen to have me back. I was all safe again, knowing I was doing the sensible thing. Hemstitching up my coffin. It was all settled."

Jinny held her breath. She could not believe that her father meant what he said. She had come so close to giving up Finmory that she could not allow herself to believe him.

"I was walking back through some of my old haunts when I saw Paula Hay. She started all this business. It was when they wouldn't listen to me and sent her to prison that I knew I had to get out. When she saw me, she recognised me. She'd a baby in a pram, an infant hanging on to her skirt. She looked straight at me, and I knew she associated me with one thing — sending her to prison. Didn't remember all I'd tried to do for her. Only one thing. I was the bloke who had sent her to prison. She didn't speak; pushed the pram straight past me. But that was it — I can't go back. You'll all need to starve, for I'm not going back to Stopton."

"But no one wanted you to go back!" cried Jinny.

"It'll not be that when you're needing things," said her father ruefully.

"It's you we need. You and Finmory. Things that don't change. Just to be there so we have something to hold on to when we need it. So that the ground doesn't move. So that we know who we are."

"What are you going to do now?" asked Mrs. Manders, smiling at her husband.

"Make pots," said Mr. Manders. "Chat with Ken. Write about the things I know — you and Petra and Jinny and Mike. Be part of the answer, not part of the mess. Be with you."

"And I was so looking forward to the supermarket."

"We won't even be able to afford Mrs. Simpson's shop," said Mr. Manders grimly. "Things will be really tight for a bit. Basic basics, and that will be all. First thing I'll start to look around for new markets for my pots. That should bring in some cash."

Jinny left them together. She went out into a world re-created, given back to her.

"We're not going," she told Shantih, still hardly able to believe it herself. "Not going. Staying here," and Jinny stared about her at moor and mountains, open sky and sea, all her own again.

And for a moment of insight, Easter cantered free, renewed, made whole again, a red rose on her forehead. She came to the wise woman, Keziah, who laid her hands on either side of Easter's head and kissed the rose.

Ecstasy sang through Jinny. She soared eagle-winged through sky-freedom of joy; was without limit or bounds.

When Mr. MacKenzie heard how nearly Jinny had drowned he shook his head at her, told her she had the luck of the tinkers to have found her way out of the current.

"I could be taking you out in the boat and showing you the exact spot where you can break free from the current. Three souls I've known taken off that headland and not one of them found the place, although they all had the knowledge of it."

The Daltons went away when Paul heard that Finmory was not for sale. Jinny didn't see Kat again. But two weeks later, when Jinny had had a postcard from Sue saying that they were going to manage a fortnight's camping at Finmory after Greece, and Mr. Manders had found an Inverburgh store with branches throughout Scotland that liked his pottery and thought they could sell as much as he could give them, there was a parcel for Jinny through the post. It was Jinny's watercolour of Shantih in a silver frame. The note with it said, "Yours — Kat."

Hardly able to believe her eyes, Jinny lifted the picture from its wrappings and stared at it with delight that was almost pain. The painting was part of herself; part of Shantih.

"'Her face is a lamp uplifted to guide the faithful to the place of Allah'," she quoted aloud. "Oh, Shantih. Shantih. Shantih."

Armada

*Another thrilling story by one of Armada's most
popular pony book authors*

THE
HORSE FROM BLACK LOCH

Patricia Leitch

Somewhere over the hills the Horse waited, its magnificent head lifted, listening...

In the great hall at Deersmalen, Uncle Vincent raised his glass in a toast. 'To the One of the Black Loch,' he said.

What is the secret of the Black Loch that the Innes family have guarded so jealously for centuries? And why does the arrival at Deersmalen of Kay Innes, with her black hair and dark grey eyes, cause such a stir?

Kay soon finds herself at the centre of an amazing adventure that leads her to the shores of the sinister Black Loch. For the Horse of the House of Innes is in terrible danger, and Kay is the only one who can ride it to safety. But, galloping through the night over the treacherous moors, can they escape from their ruthless pursuers?

Armada

CHRISTINE PULLEIN-THOMPSON

Five thrilling books by Christine Pullein-Thompson about Phantom, the beautiful, wild Palomino whom no one could capture.

PHANTOM HORSE

The story of how Angus and Jean go to America, and catch their first glimpse of Phantom in the Blue Ridge Mountains. They are determined to catch him – but so are others, whose motives are sinister . . .

PHANTOM HORSE COMES HOME

Phantom is Jean's greatest joy, but wildness is still in his blood – and when the family has to move back to England, Jean knows he'll never stand the plane journey. Halfway across the Atlantic, Phantom goes mad . . .

PHANTOM HORSE GOES TO IRELAND

A trip to Killarney with Phantom and Angus will be a wonderful holiday, Jean imagines. But it is not the peaceful place she expects. Strange noises are heard in their host's house at night – and then Angus is kidnapped . . .

PHANTOM HORSE IN DANGER

Angus and Jean devise a daring plan to rescue Angus's horse, Killarney, from a cruel horse dealer. But the plan goes horribly wrong. Terror-struck, they realise they may never see Phantom alive again . . .

PHANTOM HORSE GOES TO SCOTLAND

An idyllic Scottish island becomes a terrifying prison for Angus and Jean when they witness the kidnapping of a team of Olympic show-jumpers. Trapped by the criminals, Jean and Phantom are forced to make a dare-devil swim through rough seas in a bid to save Angus's life.

Armada

HI KIDS!
I'VE GOT THE
POWER TO BRING YOU FUN,
ADVENTURE, AND
EXCITEMENT!

Here are just some of the best-selling titles that Armada has to offer:

- [ ] **The Whizzkid's Handbook 2** Peter Eldin 95p
- [ ] **The Vanishing Thieves** Franklin W. Dixon 95p
- [ ] **14th Armada Ghost Book** Mary Danby 85p
- [ ] **The Chalet School and Richenda** Elinor M. Brent-Dyer 95p
- [ ] **The Even More Awful Joke Book** Mary Danby 95p
- [ ] **Adventure Stories** Enid Blyton 85p
- [ ] **Biggles Learns to Fly** Captain W. E. Johns 90p
- [ ] **The Mystery of Horseshoe Canyon** Ann Sheldon 95p
- [ ] **Mill Green on Stage** Alison Prince 95p
- [ ] **The Mystery of the Sinister Scarecrow** Alfred Hitchcock 95p
- [ ] **The Secret of Shadow Ranch** Carolyn Keene 95p

Armadas are available in bookshops and newsagents, but can also be ordered by post.

HOW TO ORDER
ARMADA BOOKS, Cash Sales Dept., GPO Box 29, Douglas, Isle of Man, British Isles. Please send purchase price of book plus postage, as follows:–

    1–4 Books .... 10p per copy
    5 Books or more . . . . no further charge
    25 Books sent post free within U.K.

Overseas Customers: 12p per copy

NAME (Block letters)

_____

ADDRESS

_____

_____

_____